Enjoy

Presented by:

J. Ellington Ashton Press

www.jellingtonashton.com

2019

Goddess

Goddess

By

Stuart R Brogan

Goddess

Edited by: J. Ellington Ashton Press Staff

Cover Art by: Michael "Fish" Fisher

http://jellingtonashton.com/

Copyright.

Stuart R. Brogan

©2019, Stuart R. Brogan

ALL RIGHTS RESERVED. This book contains material protected under International and Federal Copyright Laws and Treaties. Any unauthorized reprint or use of this material is prohibited. No part of this book, including the cover and photos, may be reproduced or transmitted in any form or by any means, electronic or mechanical, including photocopying, recording, or by any information storage and retrieval system without express written permission from the author / publisher. All rights reserved.

Any resemblance to persons, places living, or dead is purely coincidental. This is a work of fiction.

Table of Contents

One 8

Two 12

Three 22

Four 38

Five 48

Six 56

Seven 66

Eight 78

Nine 90

Ten 100

Eleven 114

Twelve 124

Thirteen 130

Fourteen 142

Fifteen 150

Sixteen 154

Thanks to:

Cat, Andrew & all at JEA for unleashing the beast. Jim at Wetworks for taking the plunge and getting me on board. Kitty Kane for all the help, advice and friendship. Becky Narron and all the reviewers both in print and online for giving my work a go.

My family for their continued support and of course my Wife Fiona, who is my very reason for living, I love you.

And of course, to you, the reader. Without whom I wouldn't be doing what I'm doing. If this is your first ride on the Brogan crazy train, then buckle up. If not, let's get started.

Let the blood flow……

Dedication:

Frank Michaels Errington. lover of Horror, exponent of witty banter & all-round top bloke. RIP.

Goddess

One

Steven could hear the click of her heels coming down the corridor. His body began to tense as his senses heightened. He pressed his ear against the door inwardly revelling in hearing her approaching footsteps. The excitement was building. His heart was swelling, the organ threatening to explode from his very chest. She was getting closer now. The hypnotic sound growing louder.

Even without seeing his approaching guest, Steven knew it was her. He could sense it. He could feel her aura saturate the very atmosphere around him, her sinister sexuality pulsing through brick and plaster and burrowing its way into flesh and bone. Oh, how he had yearned to meet her, to please her, to bow his head in subservient delight and worship at the altar of flesh and delectable torment. Then all was silent, as she paused outside his hotel door.

He could hear her breathing; it was soft and low, steady, and somehow hypnotic. He stepped away from the temporary barrier separating them, his body shaking with awe and anticipation for what lay ahead. The promise of redemption was seeping from his every pore. Steven couldn't help but hold his breath, for fear of alerting her to his nervous and watchful presence. He froze as she knocked three times, the pre-arranged signal for her arrival. Her knocks were gentle yet conveyed the dominance she exuded. He reached for the door and disengaged the handle.

Then, as he sucked in a staggered breath, he pulled the door open, ready to face his fate with every fibre of his existence, eagerly awaiting the chance to prove his undying devotion.

The young man was speechless, for she was indeed a Goddess, even more beautiful in the flesh than he had ever dared to envision. He had seen her in photos of course, but this was no longer the virtual world with its digital safety net. This was reality, and here she stood in all her radiance, her flesh and blood meant for both intense pleasure, and exquisite pain.

She remained silent, her body language relaxed and unmoving. Her long black hair pulled back into a tight ponytail, her lips plump and coated in vivid red lipstick, her features sublime with her make up perfectly applied. He cast his eager eyes across her body but there was little on show. She was draped in a long black coat buttoned from her knees to her throat, its collar closed with a silver dragon clasp. He suddenly caught a glimpse of her black stocking-clad legs as she shifted her weight, her feet encased in a pair of patent black heels. She said nothing as he smiled timidly and gestured for her to enter. Somehow words seemed pointless and would only sour the moment. She swooped past him without making eye contact and, as if being commanded, Steven realised he was lowering his head in reverence. He didn't feel demeaned. Not yet. That would come soon enough.

The young man gently closed and locked the door, he wanted nothing to disrupt this moment and he turned to face her. She remained silent as she slowly started to unbutton her coat. As she pulled it from her shoulders, Steven stood in awe at the sight of her short black latex dress clinging to her slim frame. The highly glossed shine and lines of the material followed and extenuated the contours of her body. He couldn't help but notice her breasts, pushed together and struggling against her garment. Once again, her dark black seamed stockings caught his eye, but this time he could see the tops attached to a suspender belt that disappeared beneath her dress. He sheepishly glanced up and their eyes met. He felt like some scolded child stood quaking before the headmistress, his knees weak with anticipation.

"Well?" She asked abruptly.

"I, I don't know what to say."

"Am I as pleasing in the flesh as you had hoped? Am I not everything you had fantasised of? More importantly, do you think you are worthy of my attentions, should I allow it?" her tone was abrasive, yet undeniably sexual.

All he could do was nod.

"Good. I'm glad you know your place, now come to me and we shall begin."

Goddess

Two

One week earlier:

"Are you listening to anything I'm saying, or are you deaf as well as stupid?"

Steven glanced up from his computer screen to see Chloe Hargreave's leering face staring down at him, her sandy blonde hair slicked back and wet looking. He squirmed in his seat at the sight of his overweight supervisor leaning forward, her body language testing the very limits of his personal space, her twenty-stone body straining at her clothing in a bid to escape and no doubt smother him to death. He feigned interest and smiled whimsically, hoping the gesture would be enough for her to just leave and hopefully never come back.

"Oh, Hi Chloe. How can I help you?"

The sneering, obese woman let out a cackle, her mouth sending a spray of spit over Stevens shoulder.

"I said, have you got those files I requested? We aren't paying you to be bone idol you know; you really are useless, aren't you? No wonder you've never had a girlfriend." she paused and looked around the open office in the hope that she had gained an audience. She had. Twelve other employees sat motionless, watching the scene before them. No one was willing to get involved for fear of becoming her next target or agreeing with her and enjoying another round of the ongoing and daily drama. Chloe grinned, their compliance fuelling her act of intimidation and returned her attention to the target of her scathing onslaught. She smiled as she began her tirade once again.

"Fucking loser, you've worked here for two years now and you still don't know what you are doing. You truly are a waste of fucking space. Why don't you grow a set of balls and be a real man for a change?"

She slammed another pile of paperwork on his desk, causing him to jump; his already nervous disposition agitated further by the ignorant fat lady and her unnecessary power-hungry display.

"Fucking do that lot, too. I want it on my desk first thing tomorrow morning, no excuses. If they are late, you can start looking for another job."

She eyed him up and down, her face red and puffy from her sustained barrage.

"But I doubt anyone would fucking have you!"

She growled under her breath and walked away. Steven couldn't help but snigger as he watched her waddle the length of the office. She vanished into the staff canteen, no doubt to steal some other worker's lunch or sacrifice a baby to her dark lord, Lucifer. He glanced up at the plain white clock on the wall in front of his desk. He let out an incredulous and laboured sigh when he saw the time was only half past two. Steven lowered his head and let it fall onto his computer keyboard, his positive feeling of self-worth all but crushed. Chloe had been right about one thing, he was a loser and, alas, it was indeed true that he had never had a proper girlfriend. Sure, there was Kelly Bower whom he dated for a week back when he was twelve, but nothing of any substance. He was a laughing stock of the office and knew damn well that he was the brunt of many a joke regarding his lack of sexual experience. To say it bothered him was an understatement, even though he tried to hide it, not that anyone bought into his lacklustre subterfuge.

Socially speaking, at twenty-one years old, he should have had a steady girlfriend by now and possibly the beginnings of an outstanding and interesting career to look forward to. But alas, again, all he had was a shitty studio flat with a damp problem and a pet goldfish named Errol. Not exactly a prize catch, by anyone's standards. Of course, he had tried to do things that, in theory, should have bumped him up the dating pecking order, but none had really panned out the way he had envisioned. He had joined his local gym, but had nearly done himself some serious injury when, while attempting a bench press, the bar and a pile of heavy weights fell on him. He really hurt his chest, much to the amusement of the resident beefed-up gym rats who, instead of helping, just pointed and laughed. After such an embarrassing foray, he decided that a more aerobic form of exercise was better for him, until he tripped and fell, breaking his ankle in front of a class of gorgeous looking, Lycra-clad women. He could still see their faces contorting with laughter at the sight of his scrawny body rolling on the floor in agony. As for the time he went indoor rock climbing, well, the less said about that, the better.

Steven dragged himself to his feet and slowly made his way to the staff toilets, desperate to snatch some respite from the pointless drudgery that was his life. He kicked open the door and entered the room, his mind all but resigning itself to the fact that the world did indeed hate him. He stared at his dishevelled reflection and sighed. He scanned the image before him: his shaggy dark brown hair and blue eyes, his thin neck and skinny frame; even his suit hung from his body as if it too hated him. It gave him a look akin to an anorexic scarecrow. No wonder he was single. What woman in their right mind would ever find him attractive? He splashed his face with cold water in an attempt to wash away the feelings of worthlessness. With another deep sigh, he turned and exited the bathroom, the soul crushing feeling of his dead-end job increasing with every step.

He slumped back down into his office chair and stared blankly at his computer screen, then to the mountain of paperwork on his desk. Steven had worked at Miller Recruitment for the last two years after being taken on from a temporary post. At the time, they had suggested that it was the start of a dazzling corporate career, he soon realised that it was anything but. In truth, he was nothing more than a glorified secretary, and he was sure that if he had actual friends, they would indeed be laughing their socks off at him, and his mediocre career choice. He would no doubt be a social pariah within his own clique. The fact that he didn't have any friends was also a source of amusement to the women in the office. He was the only male there apart from the big boss who nobody really saw. In fact, he hadn't been present for some weeks. Probably off playing golf again or lounging on his private yacht somewhere in the Mediterranean. Once again, he stared at the clock, willing it to be nearly five pm, or near to. It wasn't, it was two forty-five.

"Bollocks," he whispered to himself. The only thing he could do was plough-on and try to make it through the day. It was only Monday afternoon but at least he had booked the rest of the week off. He wasn't going anywhere, he just wanted to escape this hell-hole for a while, no matter how brief the time. If that meant sitting at home on his own, playing on the computer and watching cheesy horror DVD's, whilst eating crappy junk food, he could live with that.

At five pm Steven powered down his computer, stretched triumphantly, and got up from his desk. He cautiously looked about the office, silently praying that Chloe the slut monster, wasn't anywhere near him. He was relieved to see that she wasn't. He truly couldn't be bothered with dealing with her at this time of day. He knew that any engagement or battle of wits would surely put him in a bad mood for the rest of the evening and that really would be the perfect end to an already shitty day. For now, his mission was to escape without any drama or confrontation.

He grabbed his coat and small rucksack containing his limited-edition Batman lunch box and headed for the door. He didn't bother to take the time to say goodbye to anyone else, in fact they probably wouldn't even notice he had gone. As he finally escaped the office building, a sense of freedom washed over him. He closed his eyes and sucked in the cold autumnal air, the brisk breeze calming him.

"Bye-bye loser have a nice holiday doing fuck all with none of your mates," he heard Chloe heckle as she left the main entrance behind him. His heart sank, so much for sneaking out unnoticed he thought, as her entourage of sycophants sniggered and scoffed. He decided not to retaliate. Instead, he turned his collar up, slung his backpack, and began to make his way down the road towards the bus stop, the allure of freedom vastly more welcoming than the need to defend his shrinking masculinity.

The rush hour traffic was building up around him, the fumes and noise just a couple more things to add to his already sullen and deteriorating mood. Steven rummaged in his pocket to find his MP3 player and popped the tiny buds into his ears; at least the music would drown out the cacophony of city life and give him some semblance of peace. That was until he realised it had run out of charge. The young office worker felt like screaming at the top of his lungs.

How much more could this shitty life throw at him? Why him?

He heard the high-pitched squeal of the buses brakes and glanced up. The throng of people around him barged past, nearly knocking him to the floor, their eagerness to get aboard the public transport negating any human decency or decorum. He just let them go. The notion of any form of aggravation making him feel socially awkward, not to mention physically sick.

As he patiently waited his turn, his gaze caught sight of the neon bulbs of a cellar wine bar across the road. He huffed under his breath. In all the years of taking this route, he had never noticed a bar there before. Maybe it was new, maybe it was one of those pop-up businesses that were all the rage these days. Steven eyed the A board at the top of the descending staircase.

"Tired of life? Come in and get wasted!" it exclaimed jovially. The young man started to laugh, was this sign written especially for him? Was the universe trying to tell him something? Was this some kind of cosmic nudge perhaps?

It only took a split second for Steven to think fuck it and was already making his way amongst the traffic and across the road before he realised what he was doing. He stood motionless, transfixed by the neon sign, the lights alluring and reassuringly enticing, but that was the point wasn't it? To tempt people in and to blow their entire wage, to drown out the feeling of hopelessness. He stared at the bars name, willing it to mean something to him personally, for it to be some sort of a divine message sent from a higher realm.

"The Horny Toad," he said aloud.

Steven grimaced at his stupidity, the realisation that it wasn't some cryptic message after all and was in fact just a really oddly named drinking establishment.

"What are you waiting for young man? You know you belong in there, take the first step and see where the road leads."

Steven turned to face the corner of the steps and the direction of the unexpected address. He strained his eyes in the gloom to find the source of the voice and was taken aback by the bundle of moving boxes piled against the wall. A dirty and dishevelled face peered out from amongst them. Steven stepped forward to gain a better look at what he presumed to be a homeless man buried beneath the mound of rags and rubbish, the stench of filth and putrid urine beginning to envelope him as he cautiously edged closer.

"Excuse me, were you talking to me?"

There was a wheezy cough and a subdued throaty chuckle.

"Go on in, Sir, go on in. I'm sure you will enjoy yourself, you never know, it just might be the making of you. Let your troubles be a thing of the past."

Steven smiled meekly and chose to ignore the man, not wanting to engage in a full-blown conversation. Not only that, the air was too ripe for any more lingering.

With a deep breath he made his way down the steep flight of stairs that led to the entrance, he didn't normally drink but tonight he was feeling adventurous. It was about time he mixed things up a bit and allowed his dangerous side to come to the fore and unleash the party animal trapped within. He nodded, agreeing with his inner voice and willing himself forward. He had a new mission, and that was to get completely and utterly wasted, and to be honest, it felt bloody good.

As Steven descended into the subterranean depths, the homeless man's gaze never left him, his cold emotionless eyes watching on eagerly. He grinned a toothless smile as the wave of excitement began radiating, warming his body. As Steven disappeared, he started to giggle softly. Won't be long now, he thought to himself.

Goddess

Three

The unmistakeable aroma of stale beer and tobacco caught Steven's nostrils as soon as he entered the dimly lit bar. He found this curious as he was under the impression that smoking had been banned inside public buildings and most other spaces. Obviously, the owner of this particular establishment didn't really care for enforcing such regulations and Steven found himself giving major kudos to this anti-authoritarian stance. It would appear that there were indeed still rebels out there willing to stick their middle finger up at the world, and to hell with the consequences. He only wished he possessed such vigour and grit.

As he took in his surroundings, Steven noted that the low-ceilinged bar didn't have traditional pub seating, but what looked like ten cosy and private enclaves, strategically placed amongst low standing tables. Every one of which was furnished with a small art décor lamp, the bulbs casting a small and intimate glow upon the highly polished wooden veneer. The finishing touch was a hefty looking glass ashtray. To Steven's inexperienced eyes, the room looked more like an up market private gentlemen's club from some Hollywood film Noir as opposed to a bar found on a busy high street in the UK. Upon further inspection he could see that each table was flanked by four plush leather looking armchairs and despite giving the impression of being a tad worn, they gave the bar a sense of class and sophistication. On first impressions Steven loved it, the ambience was somewhat refined and soothing, and he felt as if he had been accepted into some sort of secret or little-known getaway, far from the bland realities of the normal world mere feet from where he now stood.

As he made his way tentatively to the bar his eyes eagerly scanned the walls, his brain taking in everything he saw, his excitement building. All available wall space was jammed with both pictures and prints of old scenes from classic movies or dark and twisted paintings. He had never seen anything like it. He stood, mesmerised by the forlorn images of twisted torsos entwined like lovers reaching up to a blackening sky. A dystopian and barren landscape with only a few highlighted white specks giving the impression of a thousand eyes staring back at the admirer. A red and distorted sun aloft a scene of humanity's ruin, it's buildings nothing but twisted iron and crumbling masonry. Steven was enthralled, the bleakness of the paintings stirring something primal within him. He had never in his life seen horrors that invoked such an aura of beauty.

"Good evening. Can I help you, Sir?"

The voice startled Steven who was still engrossed with one of the many paintings. He turned to face the smartly dressed bartender who was busy wiping a glass and smiling broadly at the new arrival.

"Um, yes, good evening," he answered with a subdued croak.

"We've never seen you in here before, you must be a newbie so as such. We bid you welcome, weary traveller." The barman gave a shallow bow.

Steven moved to the bar, sat himself down on a stool and dumped his rucksack on the floor. He shifted uncomfortably on his seat, taken aback by the unexpected, yet hearty welcome.

"Is it that obvious? Yeah, I'm new, never been in here before. In fact, I didn't know this place even existed. Got to say I really like it, it looks fantastic. I reckon this could be my local bar from now on."

The bar tender smiled and stifled a giggle as if Steven had said something amusing.

"Why thank you for the kind words, we are glad you feel compelled to visit, but of course I am sure you realise that we have always existed, we have always been here. You just haven't noticed us until now, and now being the exact time we were expecting you," he replied, somewhat cryptically.

"Well in that case, I'm glad I've found you and that I'm on time. So, what beer would you recommend for a newbie such as myself? I'm not a big drinker so any advice would be most welcome."

The bartender winked and smiled warmly, slung his bar towel over his shoulder and leaned forward. Steven couldn't help but mirror his subtle but deliberate movement.

"It would be my pleasure, Sir. If I may be so bold as to recommend our house beer, a light and refreshing beverage, yet deep in taste and full-bodied. The perfect antidote to a hard day's work, dealing with those who have no right to be breathing the same air as the likes of you and I," he stated gleefully.

"Um, that sounds perfect, cheers. I shall trust your judgement in such matters and have a pint please."

"No problem, Sir. One pint of Leviathan's Tentacle coming right up."

Steven watched as the bartender grabbed a freshly washed glass and headed towards the end of the bar to retrieve his drink. The young man stared at his host and couldn't help but admire his unusual, yet classy, dress sense. The barman was wearing a crisp white shirt, buttoned to the collar, on top of which sat a black and purple waist coat, topped off with a delicate looking silver pocket watch chain. His hair was dark black and neatly swept back, his face adorned with a well-manicured beard and thin, waxed moustache. Steven truly wished he had the grit to be so adventurous with his attire, but his self-belief had taken such a battering over the years, he just couldn't face further ridicule at the hands of his cruel work colleagues; not to mention the world at large.

As he was enjoying the moment and dreaming of how he too could pull off such a look, he was suddenly aware of someone else close to him. He turned and was shocked to see that the room was now practically full, each table occupied with at least two people. He could hear the muffled conversations interspersed with bouts of raucous laughter, the sound of glasses clinking, and cigars being lit then inhaled deeply. The new arrival looked on as all around him people were relaxing and enjoying themselves and he suddenly felt at home, as if he had found his island of tranquillity. He couldn't help but smile as the memories of his troubles began to slowly fade into insignificance. For once in his mediocre life, Steven felt accepted.

"There you go, Sir. One pint of Leviathan's Tentacle. If I may be so bold as to suggest that you sit back, enjoy, relax, and let your troubles be a thing of the past for you are indeed among likeminded folk."

Steven turned to the barman and went to retrieve his wallet from his jacket pocket.

"How much do I owe you for the pint?"

The dapper host raised his hands in protest, his face a picture of exaggerated offence.

"No, no, no, we wouldn't hear of it, Sir. The first one is on the house, a simple gift from all of us here at The Horny Toad."

"Eh? Wow, thank you, are you sure?"

The barman closed his eyes and nodded gently.

"Why of course, look about you, Sir. We are all ecstatic that you have graced our humble abode with your presence this evening. We are always pleased when a man of your calibre chooses us over the banality of other, shall we say, less welcoming establishments."

The young man began to blush. The simple gesture had meant more to him than they could possibly know. He felt humbled, yet deep down, he had a gnawing feeling of expectation, as if he had known it would happen and was somehow entitled. He turned to see that everyone in the bar had stopped what they were doing and were now facing him, their conversations muted, their glasses raised in his honour

"Welcome friend!" they cheered in unison, each of their faces the personification of genuine hospitality. Steven nervously raised his glass in response and returned his attention to the barman who was busy cleaning glasses and wiping down the counter top.

"Thanks again for the drink and warm welcome, I'm not really used to that sort of thing. I didn't catch your name by the way…"

"Fenston, Sir." He offered his hand by way of an introduction.

"Please to meet you, Sir. And yours?"

Steven took a hefty swig of his beer; the taste was indeed sublime, and he made a mental note to inform Fenston as much. He wiped his mouth on his sleeve and took the offered hand.

"Steven. My name's Steven. A pleasure to meet you Fenston. How long have you worked here? Do you own the place?"

Fenston let out a stifled giggle.

"No Steven, I am not the owner, I am merely a humble servant. I manage the place when the owner is away attending other business interests, she travels a lot you see and doesn't spend much time here. I am entrusted with the day to day running of the bar, among other duties."

"Wow must be an interesting job…" Steven took another swig of his beer. "Much better than mine," he added as an afterthought, his tone subdued.

"How so? What exactly do you do for a living, if I may enquire?"

Steven took another sip and lowered his gaze, his embarrassment evident.

"Um, nothing of note. In fact, nothing exciting nor earth shattering I'm afraid. I work for a mediocre recruitment firm just down the road. It's boring as hell and bloody awful, in fact, I hate it, I'm nothing short of an errand boy for a bunch of power-hungry women."

Fenston stopped what he was doing and leant on the bar, his posture relaxed as if truly concerned for the young man's plight.

"Then why bother to stay? One cannot moan and whine about things you yourself have the power to change in a matter of minutes. Why not throw caution to the wind and strive forth, grab life by the balls and reach out for what your heart truly desires. You must be resolute and brave, Steven. Take the first step and you will see that fate often gives more favour to those willing to work hard and make sacrifices in the pursuit of greatness…" he paused and grinned. "You may not believe me, but I can see a bright and glorious future ahead of you Steven, even if you are currently blind to the fact. I have only just met you but as far as I can see, you allow yourself to be surrounded by self-doubt and awash with the inconsequential opinions of others. You fail to acknowledge your own potential. Each of us has a part to play in this drama we call life. Some are destined for bit parts and are nothing but mere cattle, but others, such as you and I, are pre-ordained for something truly special. Something that has the power to bring real change to the world. You must adjust your mind set and begin to think like an apex predator, Steven. In your quest for success, you have to be prepared to feast upon the carcasses of those who stand in your way, to cast them down without remorse or second thought. The truth of the matter is that it's a cold harsh universe out there and it really doesn't give a toss about the little people and their mundane existences. It has always amused me that they say the meek shall inherit the earth, but I can assure you young man, nothing could be further from the truth."

Steven almost choked on his drink at the suggestion that he could make such a difference in the world. He was a nobody, what the hell could he change? His qualifications were sub average, and his CV read like the world's most boring novel. What kind of apex predator could he make in this dog-eat-dog world? The way he felt most days, a cute fluffy bunny rabbit could finish him off without breaking so much as a sweat. He decided not to answer and carried on sipping his drink, his paranoia beginning to think Fenston was having a cheap laugh at his expense.

"My most profound and sincere apologies if I have offended you, Sir," stated the barman as if he had heard Steven's very thoughts.

The young patron nodded slowly in response.

"Nah, it's all good, don't worry about it, Fenston. I'm, I'm just not used to people having faith in me, that's all. In fact, I'm not used to people actually taking any notice, let alone offering meaningful advice. I really do appreciate it. Thank you, it means a lot."

"How long do you intend to stay tonight, Steven?"

The young patron shrugged. "I've only just got here, maybe for another few drinks, or until I can't stand and have to get a taxi home. To be honest I haven't made my mind up yet, why do you ask?"

"Sorry to be the bearer of bad news old chap, but I only ask because it's nearly eleven pm and regrettably we shall be closing the doors soon. You've been at it for quite some time now. You really are loving the Leviathan!"

"Yeah yeah, very funny, that's impossible. I've only been here half an hour at most. I haven't even finished my pint yet, save the wind-ups for when I'm really pissed."

Steven turned his gaze downwards at the twelve empty beer glasses scattered around his area of the bar. He slowly turned to take in the rest of the room to see how many people remained. To his astonishment, the room was completely empty. He and Fenston were the only occupants.

"What the hell?" he mumbled under his breath, unsure if his confusion and memory loss was to be attributed to the amount of alcohol he had apparently consumed.

"At the risk of sounding like some patronising parent, you've been knocking them back good and proper this evening. I have to say that we are mightily impressed, it means that you've been enjoying yourself and we have helped in some small way to alleviate your tiresome woes. But alas, the time has come for you to be on your merry way and come again another day. I'm sure we will be seeing you again."

Despite his trepidation, Steven found himself nodding in agreement and slipped himself off the barstool. His off-kilter equilibrium caused a slight wobble as he attempted to straighten himself. He reached out to the bar to steady his rhythmic swaying.

"Bloody hell, that's mental. I didn't realise I had drank so much."

Fenston grinned jovially and made his way to the end of the bar, opened the hatch and proceeded to help Steven with regaining his balance. With his free hand, he began to gather Steven's jacket and rucksack.

"Come Sir, let's get you outside and get you some fresh air. I will stay with you until your taxi arrives; I took the liberty of calling one for you ten minutes ago, it shouldn't be long now."

"Cheers, Fenston, you're the best, but how the hell did you know where I live?"

"Why Sir, you told us, don't you remember? We all had a very interesting conversation regarding your pet goldfish and your humble abode. In fact, you had us all in hysterics with your pithy banter and razor-sharp wit. It has been most enjoyable, a veritable banquet of hilarity and earnest emotion."

"Um, no, I, I can't remember but I suppose I must have. Um, thanks again for the help. I don't normally drink so this is a bit embarrassing."

Fenston chuckled and put his arm around Stevens waist.

"Think nothing of it, Sir. That Leviathan sure does pack one hell of a wallop and when it connects, we like to go the extra mile to make sure our special customers are taken care of."

Arm in arm they made their way out of the front entrance and slowly staggered up the steep steps to the main road above.

"I'm really sorry about this, I'm..." Steven was struggling, his limbs refusing to obey his commands, his speech slurring, his mouth unable to convey the correct words to his host.

"Fucking hell, that beer has proper floored me, its bloody great stuff, thanks for recommending it."

The bartender just smiled, amused by the intoxicated patron yet his own body aching from the exertion of taking Steven's sluggish weight.

"You are most welcome, Sir. It was our pleasure."

Upon reaching the top of the steps, Steven cheered in triumph. The ascent akin to climbing the highest alpine peak, it had taken its toll, but he had emerged victorious. He straightened up and exhaled a deep breath then looked around expecting a throng of late-night activity. He tried to focus on the pile of rubbish where he had talked to the homeless man earlier that evening, but he was nowhere to be seen. Steven shrugged, the fact he had gone not bothering him in the slightest and he returned his attention to the street. He froze and rubbed his eyes at the sight that befell him. The main road was barren and strangely devoid of both traffic and people. There was no sign of human activity at all. He sucked in a deep lungful of cold air in the hope it would clear his vision, and nervously scanned from left to right. He could see nothing that he recognised. Then his gaze fell on the surrounding buildings. Steven looked on in disbelief. The structures appeared decayed and ruined. The tarmac road and pathways were cracked and overrun by weeds and impregnated with long tendrils of vicious looking thorns, all reaching out to ensnare anything that dared to stray too close. He gazed at the windows, all of which had been smashed, leaving only sinister looking shards aching to inflict injury and finally to the sign posts scattering the urban area. The twisted metalwork was splattered with what looked like dried blood and crowned with disfigured human cadavers, their faces contorted as if frozen whilst screaming for a salvation that evidently never came.

Steven suddenly felt weak, his limbs wanting to buckle under the insanity of this nightmarish delusion. He clenched his eyes tight, desperately willing the obscene images to be vanquished and replaced with happier times. His head pulsed as his mind scrambled to make sense of what was happening, the alcohol adding confusion to his already besieged senses. He felt nauseous, as if he was going to pass out, his fear starting to take hold with a vice like grip. It was then he heard the discordant and archaic noise from above, a sound akin to a distraught mammal or some other poor creature screaming in agony. He tentatively raised his head to the heavens and opened his eyes. He stared on with utter repudiation, his body shaking from a fresh wave of dread and deep seeded terror.

The sky itself was stygian black, interspersed with waves of delicate red and orange fire, their ebb and flow giving the appearance of a diseased and sinister aurora. He squinted as his peripheral vision began catching glimpses of dark shapes of varying sizes, gently swimming amongst the swirling cloud formations and putrid fumes. Their silhouettes cast monstrous shadows against choking smoke plumes rising from unseen fires, their bodies hazy but without doubt, not of this world. Large squid like tentacles hung from the fiery maelstrom, their viciously barbed tips ripping at the tops of the surrounding buildings, the impact causing large chunks of mortar to come crashing to the ground, adding to the extirpation. Steven tore his gaze away from the horror above and stared at Fenston, who appeared to be oblivious to the chaos engulfing them, his body posture calm and relaxed.

"Are you seeing this, Fenston? What the fuck is happening!" he bellowed as the ambient sounds of flame and cataclysmic torment grew louder around him, the nightmarish crescendo increasing with every passing second. Fenston remained motionless as if he hadn't heard. Steven reached out a trembling hand to rouse him from his catatonic state but as he did so, he was shocked to feel Fenston's face was freezing cold. He snatched his hand back and through tear stained eyes, once again stared at the ominous sky, as it danced seductively above him. The cacophony increased and as it did so, Steven could feel a pressure wave encircle him. His skin felt as if a million tiny needles were probing at him and he was suddenly aware of some unseen malevolent presence close by. The foul acrid stench of decay filled his nostrils, making him gag. He lowered his head and clamped both hands to his ears in the desperate hope that it would stop. He screamed as the noise grew even louder, and then it suddenly fell silent. Steven looked up to witness the sky freeze, like someone had paused a video tape. The swarm of hellish creatures were immobilised above him as if in some cosmic time shift. Their limbs twisted and contorted, their savage looking tentacles swaying gently below them. As he sucked in another ravaged breath, he began to rub his hands together, his fear almost palpable and then, as suddenly as it had stopped, it began again. This time all he could hear was a single word whispered all around him. He strained his ear to identify what was being spoken and froze as he realised what it was. Something was calling his name.

Goddess

Four

Steven woke with a jump. The sudden high-pitched burst from the alarm clock causing his body to tense and his limbs to act on reflex, as he threw his hand out to silence the intrusive noise. The impact caused the bedside table to rock back and forth, and the clock itself to tumble to the carpeted floor.

He sat up, rubbed the tiredness from his eyes, and began to take in his surroundings, unsure if he was awake or still lingering in some lucid dream state. He glanced down at his naked body, a thin film of sweat encasing him, his bedsheets damp. He propped himself up against the headboard and tried to focus. His cautious and weary stare scrutinizing the abundance of everyday objects scattered about the bedroom. He sighed deeply, relieved when everything around him appeared normal. An unexpected sensation of terror suddenly swept through him, his mind's eye vividly recalling the previous night's scene of wanton devastation and the horrific beasts that had revealed themselves to him. On impulse, he threw himself forward and jumped from his bed, desperate to see the outside world. He snatched the curtains apart, his eyes craving to see the sky, to check that his nightmare hadn't come to pass. He started to laugh uncontrollably as the world outside stared back at him. Exactly the same as it did every other day.

Everything was as it should be, but for the constant hypnotic sound of heavy rain hammering against his flimsy window. With one hand, he gently wiped the moisture from the glass and let his eyes soak up the normality beyond, his relief allowing the feelings of helplessness to subside if only for a short while.

Steven slumped back down on the edge of his bed and held his head in his hands. What the hell happened last night? Was it a dream? It surely had to be, either that or he was having some sort of mental episode. But would someone suffering from such a condition recognise as much? He stood once again, his constant state of confusion sending reoccurring waves of nausea throughout his body. He tried to steady his breathing and stretched his aching muscles, his head thumping with the rhythmic pulsing, from either the sudden wakeup call or the alcohol so eagerly and unexpectedly devoured. He padded to the bathroom and turned on the shower, the need to wash away the feelings of vulnerability and inner torment overwhelming. He gently climbed in to the cubical and stood motionless, unconcerned that the heat from the spray was stinging his skin. For what seemed like an age he stood, letting the hot water cleanse his body and mind of the horrors he had witnessed. His body shuddered involuntarily as he recalled the voice calling his name and the seductive allure of wanting to, no-needing to, answer it. He felt dirty, as if he had been spiritually assaulted by some all-devouring deity; his very soul corrupted, his eternal damnation all but assured. Try as he may he couldn't fully explain or fathom what he was feeling. The crushing sensation of desolation and terror, yet a warming feeling of acceptance and serenity. A slight smile caught his lips as the thought of absolute devotion gnawed its way into his mind, his very core yearning to submit and kneel before a starless universe, far from this world and its meaningless toils.

As he relaxed under the warming spray, his thoughts began to wonder ever deeper, slowly drifting further and further from his reality. As the darkness started to rescind, he began to see incoherent shapes twisting and morphing, their meaning incomprehensible. Then, as the shapes disappeared, they were replaced by more humanoid visions. He held his breath, for in his mind's eye, he could now see the faint outline of a figure, its arms outstretched as if welcoming him into the fold. Its feet were surrounded by a seething, writhing mass of what looked like people, but there was something different about them. No matter how hard he tried to focus, they remained hidden. Only partial bits of recognisable anatomy briefly escaping the darkness engulfing them, the sounds of perverse sexual ecstasy echoing through his cavernous subconscious.

He began to become aroused, his imagination spiralling, tumbling with the audio eroticism growing ever louder. He stared at the hypnotic mass of flesh again, desperate to indulge and share in its delights. Through the darkness, he began to see long glinting tendrils slowly entwining and probing. He stood watching in awe as they pushed against naked skin then broke through, eager to taste the soft inner tissue and organs of the bodies. The flesh pulsed and rose as the appendages explored further then finally erupted out of eye sockets and mouths to entwine once again. Steven stood enthralled by the visceral display of wanton carnage yet could feel his stomach lurch, his body wanting to wretch violently, his human repulsion pushing to the fore. He silently looked on as the sounds became a wailing of twisted choruses, instead of fear and screams of torment, they morphed into moans of ecstasy and carnal lust. The cacophony grew ever louder to the point of orgasm. Amongst his delirium he once again heard his name being called, it was faint at first but then grew in volume and intensity. He tried desperately to focus on the voice, he craved it. And then there it was, the unmistakable voice of a woman, a voice he had heard on the wind the night before. He smiled at the thought of her, her scent, her body, her embrace. Steven didn't know who she was but felt drawn to her sensual and seductive tone. Whoever she was, she presented herself as a vision of cosmic divinity.

"I hear you…" he whispered softly. "What do you want of me?"

She didn't reply. He desperately called out again, but her image started to fade from view. Steven held out his hand in an attempt to reach her, to guide her to him, but it was of no use. She had retreated back into the blackened void of nothingness, the mass of entwined bodies and tentacle-infused gore following close behind her.

Steven came to lying in a heap in the cubical, his legs pulled tight to his chest, the shower above him still spewing forth hot water, the room steamy and dripping with condensation. He struggled to his feet, his body shivering despite the temperature. He glanced down to see what appeared to be a large pool of blood swirling down the plughole, the grubby dull white tiles splashed with his crimson life force.

"What the fuck is happening to me?" he pleaded, his body beginning to shake violently, his face a masterpiece of sorrow and confusion.

It took a full hour before Steven could summon the strength to move from the shower. He gently checked his body for signs of self-induced injury but was relieved to find no such wound. He slowly dressed and poured himself a cup of strong coffee in the hopes it would rein his subconscious in from the furthest regions of delusion and back to reality, far away from the mysterious woman and her apocalyptic premonitions. Try as he might, it was of little use, he somehow knew at his very core that something was happening to him. He was in little doubt that he was changing, morphing into something unrecognisable, his body an unwilling vessel for the unspeakable. Steven went cold, the sudden realisation of being twisted for some others' pleasure seeping deep into his very marrow. Bit by bit, it eroded his will to fight and need to retain his own identity.

As he sipped his coffee, he struggled to make sense of his rapid descent into madness. To rationalise the onslaught of mixed emotions coursing through his mind, each clawing for supremacy and the right to prevail. And then it occurred to him that it had all started when he had entered that bar. The cryptic warning from the homeless man, the pictures on the wall depicting abominations from unseen worlds, the strange atmosphere. It was as if his mind was recreating the scenes from the artwork and projecting them, making them appear real. Maybe it really was in his head after all and had triggered some previously undiagnosed condition. As far as he could tell, there was only one course of action open to him; he had no choice but to go back and see for himself, to find the answers. He pulled on his jacket, grabbed his bag and moved to the front door then stopped abruptly. He looked down at the black and red envelope lying on his door mat, his name artistically written on the front, the wording exquisite.

Steven reached down and retrieved the unexpected correspondence. The paper felt coarse and by the looks of it, very expensive, traditional and obviously handmade. He turned it over and could see that instead of it being sealed like any normal modern envelope, it had been diligently finished off with a bright red wax seal, a single letter "M" carefully embossed into it. He huffed under his breath, could this day get any stranger? He very rarely received mail, let alone anything like this. Steven dumped his bag on the floor and threw his jacket to one side. Before he ventured out, he had to tend to other priorities. He made his way to his little kitchen table and retrieved a small knife from the work side drawer, eager to cast his eyes over the message the envelope contained. He slid the blade between the paper and seal and gently prized it open, taking care as not to damage whatever resided within, his curiosity peaking as he unravelled the outer layer.

Inside was a single slip of high-class paper, red in colour with another "M" printed on it. Other than that, the only writing was that of a website address. He inspected both sides but found nothing else.

"What the hell?" he muttered as he read the address.

www.kneelbeforethealtarofflesh.com

Steven hesitated for a second then found himself moving swiftly to his living space and firing up his laptop. He stared blankly at the screen, willing the machine to work faster, his impatience beginning to simmer. He drummed the keyboard in frustration, desperate to find out the meaning behind the cryptic message then let out an audible sigh of relief as his search engine page flashed up, ready to fulfil his cyber command. He snatched up the red paper and typed in the website address; he looked on helplessly as the page began to load and then grinned when it appeared to load fully.

The initial home page was black with no visible writing or menu. Steven dragged his cursor around the page in the hopes of finding some hidden menu but there was nothing but blank space. He cursed under his breath at the futility of his endeavours and slumped back on his couch, eyeing the empty screen with a mixture of genuine confusion and contempt. A sudden high-pitched ping alerted him to an incoming message, which was strange as he had no other pages open, not even his email account. Steven suddenly noticed that two words had appeared in the centre of the otherwise empty screen. He glared at them, unsure of how to proceed.

Welcome friend.

Steven leant forward and perched himself on the edge of his couch, his heart rate beginning to increase, his body shaking with trepidation. He scratched his chin and carefully began typing his response.

Who are you?

There was a slight pause before another message appeared in place of his own.

Someone who can give you the answers that you seek, Steven. You only need ask.

Even more intrigued, he took in a sharp intake of breath and for a split second debated whether he should carry on with the conversation. Who the hell was this person? Could it be cyber hijackers out to freeze his computer and files until a ransom had been paid? After all, you hear of such cases all the time on the news. But if that was the case, why him? He wasn't exactly loaded with cash and he was no one of any real consequence in the greater scheme of things. He shook his head, dismissing the scenario altogether not just because it was farfetched, but because it didn't explain the visions and loss of time he had been experiencing.

What do you want from me? What answers?

The computer pinged again but instead of a direct reply, another web address appeared, and judging by the code, it was only to be found on the Dark Web. He knew this to be a secret and sinister portal to illicit trades and services the likes of which "normal" people wouldn't need or be curious. A new message followed the address.

Download TOR. Follow the link @ 2100hrs tomorrow. You will only be given one chance. Don't squander the opportunity given.

As soon as Steven read the instructions, a clock was suddenly illuminated, the numbers counting down from one minute. He leapt to his feet and darted to his desk; he grabbed a pen and paper and returned quickly to scribble down the information. He had just finished when the clock reached zero and the website link was severed, plunging his computer into total darkness.

The somewhat confused young man eased himself back into his couch and tossed the cryptic note to the floor, the beginnings of a headache clawing at his forehead. He rubbed his eyes, the pressure sending instant shockwaves cascading down his optic nerves and deep into his brain. He winced at the sudden stabbing pain. For what seemed like an eternity he sat there motionless, his eyes clenched tightly shut, willing the pain to leave him, his mind trying to grasp the situation he found himself in. When he finally opened his eyes again, the flat was in darkness, the cold florescent glare of a street lamp shining through his window was the only light source. He sighed and gazed at the rain gently bouncing off the glass. Yet again he had lost time. He must have dozed off and spent the entire day sleeping, which to be fair wasn't a bad thing. His body was feeling depleted and exhaustion was ever looming like the proverbial black dog.

He stared vacantly at the window, his vision clouded by a heavy mix of optical pain and the rain gently rolling down the glass. After all he had endured, it was obvious that his options were limited and on reflection he had made up his mind. Tomorrow he was going to follow that link and see where it led, regardless of the consequences. But before that happened, he was going to revisit that bar and get some answers.

Five

"I want to know what the fuck is going on and I want to know now!"

Fenston stared blankly at the increasingly irate customer and remained motionless. Steven slammed his clenched fist on the bar counter in frustration, the impact adding gravitas to his demand. He was shaking, his temper starting to get the better of him.

"I'm damn sure you know what I'm talking about Fenston: the messed-up pictures, the visions…"

The bartender just shrugged dismissively.

"I do apologise, but I am not quite sure I understand what you are referring to, Sir. Could you be a tad more specific please? If you would like to remain calm and slow your breathing, I'm sure we could find solutions to your current, and obviously, pressing dilemma. What say you?"

"Don't play games, Fenston. Ever since I walked into this bloody bar my life has started to take a fucking nose dive into outright insanity. I know damn well you've got something to do with it, just tell me what the hell is going on." He paused, unsure of how to proceed regarding the woman in his dreams and the surreptitious computer message.

"Who is the woman? What do you know of the Dark Web? And what is the altar of flesh?" he asked quietly. His temper subsided slightly, replaced by increasing curiosity with more than a hint of desperation.

Fenston smiled broadly, his face full of what appeared to be relief and amusement.

"Judging by the abundance of your rather curious and cryptic questions, am I correct in saying that the good lady has indeed contacted you already? Because if that is the case, it is most gratifying news, Sir. In all honesty, none of us expected her to approach you for some time. You must be truly excited about seeing her, are you not? I trust you have been invited to gaze upon her website? In truth I am so jealous of you, oh to cast my eyes upon her for the first time once again. You are indeed in for an experience of cosmic proportions."

Steven could only huff in response, somehow knowing Fenston was speaking sense yet not fully comprehending the meaning or how it related to him. Fenston clapped his hands together and raised his eyes to the heavens as if thanking some deity high above.

"Why this is marvellous news, Sir. I am of the opinion that we should indulge in a pint to celebrate this auspicious time. Come, let us take libation!"

Steven looked on as the bartender made his way to the end of the bar and began to pull two pints. He couldn't fully rationalise what was happening. It would appear the woman was indeed real after all, and Fenston had been privy to the secret all along. What's more, it was now obvious that it was her behind the clandestine note and web chat. But to what end still alluded him.

The dapper barman returned and placed the two glasses on the counter and gestured for the younger man to have a seat. Begrudgingly, Steven did as he was instructed and took a swig from his glass, more eager than ever to hear what his host had to say, but playing it cool none the less.

"You may or may not believe what I am about to tell you Steven, only the very few can fully comprehend the magnitude of the situation you now find yourself part of. All I ask is that you listen with an open mind and form your own judgement. Trust your instincts. The truth is never easy to hear, let alone understand."

Fenston paused as if waiting for permission to continue his story. Steven remained silent.

"She is not just any normal woman, my inquisitive friend. But I have a suspicion you are already aware of that fact. For you see, she is a divine Mistress and she is most certainly as real as you and I. A sublime creature of universal beauty from parts unknown and you should be honoured that she has chosen to reveal herself to you. You are a very special man indeed. Not many have seen her. Those who have, very rarely speak of it for fear of losing favour, as with any who rules over others, she can be a fickle Mistress. Especially when one of her disciples displeases her."

Steven remained silent for a few moments then slowly began to let out a stifled giggle, swiftly followed by a more wholesome and hearty laugh. His face turned a shade of red as tears began to roll down his cheeks.

"I'm sorry, hang on, I'm, I'm…"

The barman looked on as Steven struggled to engage in conversation, his words lost amongst waves of laughter. It took a few minutes for Steven to calm himself and continue.

"Just what the hell are you on about? Have you lost your fucking mind? Disciples?" He gasped between breaths.

"She's a bloody pseudonym on a web forum at best, probably some overweight house wife having fantasy issues."

Fenston looked on, unimpressed by Steven's disrespectful outburst. Despite his inward annoyance, he remained calm and continued.

"In this world, some would call her a professional dominatrix, a mistress who has the power to show you your deepest sexual and psychological desires. The power to set you free from worldly restraints and social dogma. The power to let you explore the very limits of sexual gratification, and as mere slaves to her desires, we only know of her as such. She is a seer. A dark witch of sorts. She uses the powers of the left-hand path to bring illumination to man's carnal recesses, that have, for centuries, been shrouded in darkness by religious indoctrination and the fear that some omnipotent God will cast you down into the fire for exploring such delights. Those of us who serve are truly enlightened and her mere touch is enough for the strongest of men to become not just enslaved, but to welcome it with open arms. To kneel before her is a privilege few are awarded."

Steven gently toned down the laughter. In some bizarre and twisted way, things were starting to make some sort of sense. But then again, perhaps it was nothing more than some elaborate ruse. Was it possible that this woman, or Fenston, had slipped him some sort of psychotropic drug in the hopes that he would become subservient, thus taking up the mantle of her newest slave either on line or in the flesh? Some sort of confidence trick to fleece him of his savings? As far as he could tell it was no less plausible than some esoteric witch casting spells and indulging in orgies. He glanced down at his pint glass, his paranoia willing him to inspect the contents.

"OK Fenston, I will play along. Let's say for one minute that I actually believe you. What does she want from me? I have no money, in fact, I'm pretty much broke, so what could I possibly have that she would be interested in?"

Fenston shrugged his shoulders.

"I am but a mere servant, Sir. I can no more predict her motivations any more than an ant predicts why it gets crushed underfoot. It is not our place to question or analyse the "whys" and "hows" of her decisions. We are just content in the knowledge that we are indeed part of her grand and magnificent plan."

"Which is?"

"You surprise me, Steven, haven't you figured that out for yourself yet? Why to bring perpetual order to intolerable chaos of course. To release humanity from the constraints that have held us in bondage since time began.

The barman gestured the room, his smile radiating with joy.

"A utopian world awaits all of us my friend, far removed from religious hatred and the bigotry that divides us as a species, and do you know what would be the most glorious thing about it? It is that the likes of you and I that shall be on at the ground floor from the very start. As her devoted followers, we will be privy to front row seats and will witness the glorious change that will unite humanity under a single banner. Imagine a world where no one goes hungry, a world where war is a thing of the past, would that not be something to behold?"

Steven took another hefty swig and stared coldly at his host. He gently placed his glass on the counter and nodded slowly.

"Excuse my ignorance and overt cynicism but I'm not too clued up on this whole occult thing, Fenston. Am I correct in thinking that you lot are some kind of devil worshipping cult? Is your grand plan nefarious in nature?

Do you intend to lure me into the inner circle then sacrifice me in some twisted and bloody ritual or are you just a bunch of good old fashioned mental religious fanatics harping on about the end of days, happy to drink the cool-aide handed to you by some deranged fetish model or frumpy housewife? You asked me to listen with an open mind, but from what I have heard, you and your mistress are into some pretty fucked up stuff, and I for one don't want any part of it. I'm not like you and nor do I wish to be. I'm out of whatever "IT" is and nothing you can say will change my mind."

It was Fenston's turn to laugh uncontrollably. He started to clap his hands together in childlike amusement.

"My dear Steven, but you are already part of it! Your fate is sealed and I'm afraid there is no escaping it. She has allowed you to cast your eyes upon her and there is no going back, no returning to your former life full of its mindless distractions and stifling rules. The only way forward is indeed forward, to explore and indulge, to venture forth and reimagine yourself." He paused and jabbed a well-manicured finger at the younger man. "And you are most certainly wrong Steven, for you see, you are like us."

Steven grimaced, the bartender's self-assurance becoming overbearing.

"You will see for yourself and understand when you kneel before the altar of flesh," he added smugly.

Steven stood and turned on his heels, his patience all but gone. He moved briskly to the door, eager to remove himself from the bartender's presence.

"You will see for yourself, Steven..."

Steven ignored him and tugged open the heavy entrance and headed out into the chilly night air.

"...And believe as we do..." Fenston called after him as he vanished from sight.

Six

Steven hadn't slept much that night, not just because of his infuriating conversation with Fenston, but more so the visions of obsidian skies that had plagued his dreams. He had watched on helplessly as colossally deformed beasts silently roamed murky and litter-swept streets, their orb-like white eyes searching for prey. He had seen rag draped survivors encrusted with filth and excrement huddled together amongst squalor and human remains for fear of being found outside alone. Their numbers gave false hope of survival against the cruelty that stalked them. He had gazed in terror as unfathomable and unholy horrors swam through cataclysmic clouds of pollution and smoke, high above the remnants of human endeavour. And at the centre of this horror, the image of a solitary woman, orchestrating the ruination of humanity from a throne on high.

Feeling desolate, Steven drained the dregs from his sixth mug of strong coffee and scratched the stubble on his cheeks. His face felt gaunt and withdrawn, his jaw aching from the constant grinding of teeth. He glanced at the digital clock on his laptop and could see it was three pm. Only another six hours and he would have more answers, or at least be one step closer to the truth, whatever that may be. As he stared at the screen, he began to study his own reflection, his eyes sullen and red from lack of sleep and his skin dry and pasty white in colour. He looked away, inwardly disgusted by his appearance, his personal disdain growing more prevalent with each passing moment. Steven had been analysing everything the bartender had told him, and for hours had tried to rationalise the past few days and the predicament he now found himself in. The only solid conclusion he had come to was that the woman in his visions was most certainly real and that she was indeed the catalyst for his misfortunes. Other than that, he couldn't be sure what was reality or some lucid dream state. He truly hoped that, in some part, he was losing his mind. The alternative meant that the abominations he witnessed were in fact not projections of his own subconscious, but living breathing entities, hell-bent on utter destruction.

He shuddered as he recalled his nightmares, and again, the feelings of hopelessness washing over him. Yet, despite his fears, there was something else bothering him and that was the crushing and unrelenting sensation of shame. Regardless of the terrors he had witnessed, he knew deep down that he was starting to crave her attention and was aware of the growing need to kneel before her, and he hated himself for it. Steven was used to the intolerable sensation of self-loathing, the feeling of detesting certain aspects of his own personality, its flaws and weaknesses, but this was entirely different. It wasn't your run of the mill cry for help or blatant attempt at procrastination, but an all-encompassing desire to pass over and leave this realm, the emotional reality of failure too much to bear. The fact of the matter was, some part, if not the biggest part, was actually enjoying the whole descent into reckless oblivion. It was as if it gave some meaning to his life, a feeling of being part of something greater. House wife, or mistress, it mattered not, he craved her none the less.

He psychologically shook his head, his reason and humanity trying to fight the ever-increasing need for subjugation. He got to his feet and made his way to the kitchen, the promise of another coffee giving him momentary distraction from his continuous inner turmoil. Upon returning to his living area, Steven placed the steaming mug on his small table and slumped back into his couch, the soft embrace instantly relaxing his body. He closed his eyes, the desire for sleep overcoming him. It was only a matter of minutes before he was in dreamless slumber.

Steven woke with a jump, but this time not due to the invasive high pitch bleep from his alarm clock but of his computer firing up and whirring into life. He rubbed his eyes and tried to focus on the time. 20:45 hrs. He made his way to the bathroom and splashed his face with cold water in an attempt to clear his lethargy, then made yet another coffee. He had a feeling it was going to be a long night and felt it prudent to be prepared. As he stared at his lap top, he couldn't help but continuously swap his gaze between the screen and the clock, his mind mentally counting down the minutes. He had already downloaded the necessary software to gain entry to the Dark Web and had primed his search engine with the address given. All he had to do now was wait for the allotted time and press enter. For what seemed like an age, Steven sat silently waiting. With every passing second his mind tumbled and twisted with limitless scenarios. At precisely nine pm, Steven hit the Enter button, sat back, and prepared himself for whatever was going to be revealed.

The screen went black. In fact, there was nothing visible giving any indication that he was even on the correct site. He grumbled softly, silently hoping it wasn't a dead end or some practical joke. Then slowly, an image began to morph into focus. Steven stared at the picture before him. The image was of a highly decorated wooden throne, the legs and arms expertly carved into what appeared to be the same floating entities he had witnessed in his visions. Their bodies contorted and otherworldly, their faces and mouths grotesque and infused with razor sharp teeth. The high back and seating area of the chair was carefully upholstered with lush red velvet, tacked down with shiny brass rivets to keep it all together and give the presence of regal opulence. Behind the main image, a swirling animated scene of blackening skies and lightning began to dance and swirl, every now and then giving way to graphic images of people kneeling, their bodies naked and bloody. Over and over they would suddenly appear then vanish, leaving the images burnt upon the retinas. Steven looked on, unable to look away, captivated by the dance macabre. He dragged his finger across the mouse pad and let the arrow hover over the throne then clicked the button, his motions running on instinct and eager to proceed. The page suddenly changed, and a message appeared welcoming him to the altar of flesh. He sucked in a staggered breath and began to explore the page further. It was then he first caught sight of the Mistress.

In the centre of the screen was a picture of the most beautiful woman he had ever laid eyes upon, seated on a velvet throne. Her body was encased within a long black latex dress, her straight black hair draping over her shoulders and down to her breasts. He surveyed the image even further: her long legs crossed, her feet adorned with patent black heels. He swallowed gently as he noticed the sinister looking riding crop resting across her lap. As he looked on, a message box revealed itself below the main picture and as he watched, someone began to type.

Hello Steven, welcome to the altar of flesh. I am so glad you could make it.

Steven's heart missed a beat, his excitement at fever point. "Holy shit, it's her," he found himself mouthing silently. Despite his hands shaking, he began to type his response.

Thank you. You are so beautiful, who are you?

I have many names, some as old as time itself, but you may call me Mistress.

Steven didn't know how to respond, the questions he had intended to ask all but fleeting memories, lost to a whirlpool of carnal desire, all he could do was feel humbled that he was allowed the privilege to talk to her.

What do you want from me, Mistress? How can I help you?

There was a slight pause.

My only wish is that you serve me unconditionally, Steven. To give yourself unto me and offer willingly all that you are, to become my slave, to fulfil me in any way I see fit. For this gift I shall bestow great pleasures upon you, and together, we shall explore the outer regions of nothingness. Normal people have no idea of the beauty contained within the darkness. Is this something that fills you with joy? Do you yearn for such a privilege? Tell me why I should allow you to kneel before the altar of flesh and I shall make my judgement.

Steven felt as if his body had been drained of all energy and rational emotion. His only remaining desire was to now win favour with the Mistress and for her to welcome him into her loving embrace. As of this moment nothing else mattered in his life and he was prepared to give up everything to worship at the altar of flesh. It was his destiny to serve her, any thoughts of cataclysmic annihilation or harbingers of ripped flesh were no longer his concern. He reached out to type his response then suddenly paused, the possibility of writing the wrong thing causing him to second guess his answer. He let out a breath and began to type.

Because I am nothing without you.

He sat back and waited for her response. He tapped his foot nervously, the seconds feeling as if aeons had passed. His eyes never left the screen for fear of missing some urgent command, the very real possibility of being rejected overbearing. Steven rubbed his eyes and as he did so, heard the ping of notification. He stared at his Mistress's response.

A true statement Steven and I agree, you are indeed nothing, but before I grant you your wish you must first pass two tests. If you are successful, I shall allow you to worship me. However, I must warn you that I don't take failure well. Do you understand? Are you willing to do as I command without hesitation? Are you willing to do whatever it takes to kneel before the altar of flesh? If you say yes, then there is no going back.

This time Steven didn't pause to consider his reply. His mind was resolute.

I swear to obey your commands. What would you have me do to prove my devotion?

The response was almost immediate, a response that filled him full of wonderment.

All in good time, Steven. But for now, I grant you access to my site. Explore and enjoy the delights on offer and imagine yourself with me in the flesh. I shall contact you tomorrow. Remain indoors and speak of this to no-one.

The page suddenly changed to reveal an inventory of links to video clips and photographs, each appearing to depict more extreme themes than the last. Steven found himself nodding in agreement and began to click on the links provided in turn. The first clip was of a naked man bound to a vicious looking metal chair, his head obscured by a leather mask resembling a dog. The room around him bright white and sterile akin to a hospital room. The man was silent but for a few muffled grunts and groans. Steven was mesmerised by the scene, the eroticism growing within him. It was then that the mistress appeared in front of the camera, her long black hair pulled up into a bun, her body dressed in what looked like an exaggerated and overtly sexual latex nurse's uniform. She turned to the camera and smiled, her bright red lip stick glimmering under the bright florescent glow above her. She moved towards the seated man, her patent white high heels snapping against tiled flooring as she advanced towards her quarry. Never in his life had Steven been attracted to BDSM or extreme pornography but this was beginning to stir something within him, a lust he never knew existed nor wished to explore, until now.

He swallowed hard as he watched the mistress bend over, extend her arm and start to scratch her slave's chest with her long nails, causing blood to slowly flow from the savage looking wounds. The bound man could only groan with a mix of, what Steven assumed, was ecstasy and pain. The mistress turned and smiled once again at the camera, her lips curling at the corners, her eyes wide with pleasure and feral desire. Steven couldn't take his gaze from the screen, his curiosity and arousal gaining momentum with each passing frame. He watched on, wishing he himself was there and participating.

The mistress walked off camera then returned a few seconds later carrying what looked like a rolled-up length of tightly bound leather. She released her grip slightly and let the end fall to the floor. The young voyeur gasped as he realised that it was a whip, the body of which was laced with tiny razorblades from tip to near enough the handle. Once again, the mistress grinned at the camera and with a sudden, and expertly crafted movement, swung the whip around her head and at the apex of the arc, flicked her wrist causing the tip to lash out remorselessly at her slave. The room was suddenly awash with screams as the razor blades effortlessly tore flesh from muscle. Sprays of blood erupted from the vicious wounds, sending a cascade splashing against the surrounding tiles and walls. The mistress laughed as her perfect makeup was dotted with tiny specks of her victim's body and fluids. She lashed out again and again, each time inflicting even greater injury, the cacophony of agony growing ever louder. The clip ended with the mistress standing in full frontal view of the camera, her white dress soaked in blood, her hair dishevelled and hanging loose. Steven dared not break her gaze. She stared at the camera and gently licked her lips. Steven could almost taste the blood for himself.

And so, it went on. For the remainder of the night Steven watched clip after clip. He witnessed naked men and women hung upside down from wooden crosses, their genitals and bodies mutilated with surgical implements, their flesh carved from their squirming torsos. He watched on as twenty people engaged in a gore-soaked orgy at the feet of his mistress while she sat on her throne, her gaze never leaving the camera despite the scene of debauchery playing out before her. He had seen breathing deprivation and clips of rubber clad people dressed as animals and creatures from another world engaging in extreme sexual acts, the likes of which he hadn't known existed. But far from being horrified, Steven was not only aroused but intoxicated. He yearned to be part of it, to experience the delights his mistress had to offer and as long as he fulfilled her wishes, he too would soon be part of it. He smiled, whatever she wanted him to do, he would do willingly and with an open heart.

In the early hours of the morning Steven finally climbed into his bed, his mind full of the sights he had witnessed. Nothing had ever affected him in such a way nor stirred such passion. It was if someone had lifted a veil from his eyes and granted him a new lease of vision, the vision to see all earthly pleasures at once and the opportunity to make them a reality. He curled himself into a ball as if he was an excited child waiting for Christmas day to arrive and smiled softly, desperately willing himself to sleep. Her next correspondence couldn't come soon enough.

Seven

Steven's heart jumped as he heard the dull thump of something being pushed through his letterbox and landing on his door mat. He rushed to his door, his excitement causing him to feel light headed. He almost whooped for joy as he stumbled on his bag and reached down to snatch up the small envelope. Again, it was hand made with the now eagerly anticipated "M" embossed within a red wax seal. He tried to calm himself and returned to his living area where he had his small knife primed and waiting. Once again, he diligently opened the note and began to read the contents, his eyes furiously darting over the words, taking care to consume every single instruction.

Hello Steven. Congratulations for making it thus far. For your first test I require that you go to a local hardware store and purchase two hammers, then attend St Benedict's church this evening at 1900 hrs. At this time, the church will be holding a service and I expect there to be at least one dozen people in attendance. Once there, you will sit and wait for twenty minutes, then at 1921 hrs I expect you to stand and kill as many as you can. Use the hammers, enjoy the sensation of liberation. Once you have completed this task, leave and return home and wait for me to contact you again. I will be watching, Steven. I expect nothing less than complete capitulation if you are to pass the test.

Steven beamed broadly. There would have been a time he would have felt sick at the very suggestion of inflicting pain on someone, let alone killing them. But those days were very much a thing of the past. He was a new man, a man with a sense of purpose, a man with a destiny to fulfil and if the cost of that was the extermination of a few hypocritical strangers, then so be it. The way he saw it, they were nothing more than a means to an end. Without the bludgeoning sensation of guilt or remorse, it was amazing what mankind could do, their cruel actions levied against other living beings. Some may very well judge his own actions barbaric, but he took some semblance of solace in the fact that his actions served a higher purpose, not just a mere fleeting moment of self-satisfaction. All that mattered now was succeeding and winning favour, assuring his place by her side.

He glanced at the clock. It was ten in the morning. He had plenty of time. Maybe he should relax a little before he implemented stage one of the plan. Maybe he should go to see Fenston and have a drink to eradicate any nerves or self-doubt that still lingered. Steven grinned and decided to pay the bar a visit, of course he wouldn't be able to divulge anything to do with today's activities. For all he knew Fenston may very well report back to his mistress, thus scuppering any plans of future inclusion and to Steven, that was unacceptable and completely out of the question. He got to his feet and grabbed his jacket. He didn't rush for there was no need to. Time was, for once, on his side. Feeling revitalised and galvanised with a new-found sense of optimism, he retrieved his keys and wallet then headed for the door and unlike the Steven of old, not once did he question the morality of his mission.

Steven entered the bar and noticed only a handful of people, all sat quietly nursing their drinks. The ambient sound of smooth jazz playing over the PA system adding to the serene and laidback atmosphere. He made his way to the bar and took his usual seat.

"And what can I get you today, fine Sir?" Fenston asked without looking up.

"The usual please, Fenston. Believe it or not I'm in a bloody good mood today and have a feeling things are finally on their way up. My life has turned a corner and the future is indeed bright."

The barman flashed his signature smile and grabbed two glasses.

"Well then, I guess I shall join you in celebratory libation, Sir," he replied as he made his way to the pump.

Steven took off his jacket, dropped it at his feet and rubbed his eyes, the images from his nights viewing still burnt upon his retinas, his mind replaying the scenes over and over again. He grinned and felt the now accustomed twinge within his trousers. He adjusted himself, not wanting to alert any of the bar's customers to his unexpected arousal, but the fear of detection secretly adding to the sexual thrill.

Fenston returned and placed two pint glasses on the bar and pushed one towards his patron.

"There you go, Sir, one pint of the usual and believe me when I say that I'm glad things are on the up for you, rest assured that I shall ask no questions regarding your new-found zest for life. Of course, should you need to talk things over, my ears are here for the bending."

Steven smiled and grabbed the glass, his thirst suddenly aching to be quenched. He looked around and had the sudden sensation that something was different with his surroundings. He began to scrutinise the interior, unsure of what he was feeling or what he was looking for. It was then he noticed that the bar looked somewhat shabby. The paintwork appeared to be peeling from the walls, the plaster on the roof cracked and bubbling from moisture and the onslaught of damp, and as he breathed in, even the air itself tasted foul and musty. Steven lowered his gaze to the bar counter and it too looked worn and had lost its shine. The veneer looking tatty and in need of replacing. Steven couldn't recall the place looking so dishevelled during his past few visits. In fact, he was always of the impression that it was decorated to a high standard but now something had changed, as if time itself had suddenly caught up and had lashed out with a vengeance, demanding reciprocity for sins committed. He looked up and to his surprise also noticed something odd about his usually well-groomed host. Fenston's eyes now appeared sunken and shallow, his face discoloured and blotchy, his hands and nails dirty. Fenston smiled meekly as if sensing something was amiss.

"I trust everything is ok, Steven? You seem to have lost a little colour in your complexion? You look like something is bothering you? For someone, who, just moments ago was in such a good mood, why the long face all of a sudden?"

Steven couldn't help but notice Fenston's teeth were now blackened with decay, permanently stained with what seemed to be grime and neglect. Steven rubbed his eyes and was unsure how to respond. Maybe he was just tired, the nights fun filled activities giving way to exhaustion and a heavy induced body slump. He gently shook his head.

"Nah, not at all. I can assure you everything is okay here, mate. Life is damn good now, just knackered I reckon; nothing a good kip wouldn't cure."

Fenston remained motionless, his eyes scrutinising the younger man. He raised his hand and with his finger beckoned Steven to lean in closer, the smell from his breath causing Steven to recoil slightly.

"I trust that all of your previous misgivings are now a thing of the past and that you have come to terms with our Mistress and her ways? Perhaps you have even cast your eyes upon her website and have viewed her in all of her glory, no doubt eager to get involved?"

Steven couldn't help but give away his adulation and nodded. Fenston gave a wink as if understanding what he was going to say next.

"Is it so obvious? Indeed. I have Fenston, and I think that I owe you an apology. At first, I had my doubts, but I have to admit that you were most certainly correct about seeing her for what she truly is. She is without a doubt the most beautiful creature I have ever seen and a Mistress whom I intend to serve as long as she will have me. You will be pleased to know that I now fully comprehend what you were talking about and to answer your question, yes, I have now had the pleasure of seeing her at work, and all I can say is that she truly is an artist."

Both men began to chuckle softly, each casting appraising glances over their Mistress in their mind's eyes.

"You know what? I really have to thank you for all you have done for me these past few days, Fenston. This place, and you of course, have been an absolute god send for me. It would appear you arrived just when I needed you the most, a time when I was at my lowest ebb and you could say that you have been a beacon in the darkness." Steven raised his glass in toast.

"To The Horny Toad, to you Fenston and most of all, to the Mistress!"

Fenston gently tipped his glass in response and took a sip from the beer, his predatory and questioning eyes never leaving his customer. He quietly chuffed under his breath.

"Well that is good news, Sir, but I can assure you that God had nothing to do with it." Fenston's tone was low and deliberate and somehow it made Steven feel more than a little nervous. Maybe Fenston was jealous? Maybe the realisation of another man getting close to his Mistress was a source of contention? Regardless of the reason, Steven was damn sure that the mistress favoured him over some meagre barman and as such, was determined to prove her correct in trusting him. He had every intention of fulfilling his mission that evening and moving on to the second test, of which he was confident he would also pass with flying colours.

"So, then my young friend, how would you like the Mistress to punish you? What games are you eager to play? Does Sir have a preference?"

The sudden slew of questions caught Steven by surprise and in truth he hadn't really thought about it. He was a newbie to such pursuits and didn't know where to begin. He suddenly felt embarrassed by his lack of experience. Fenston smirked sardonically as if enjoying watching the younger man squirm.

"Now now, Sir, no need to be shy or play coy, we are all friends here. Just let your mind wander and reveal to her your deepest fantasies, she will help you to reach a state of complete satisfaction as long as you are truthful with her. Remember, nothing is taboo when one is in her company, just open up and be free from guilt, the pleasures she can give you are only limited by your own imagination."

"I, I haven't really given it much thought to be honest, I liked what I saw on the clips."

Fenston chuckled.

"Aaahhh, and what could that have been, I wonder. Is it possible that it was the sight of auto erotic asphyxiation? Or the barbed and brutal lashing and flogging? Could it be the prospect of the St Andrews cross, of which you are to be bound and emasculated for her pleasure? Perhaps yours is more to do with the visual stimuli, the texture and smell of heavy latex and rubber. Is that more to your liking, Steven? The sensual texture of the material against naked virgin flesh? But a word of caution, my friend, with such little experience pleasing a woman, make sure you don't stumble and fall at the first hurdle and leave our Mistress wanting. I don't think you could cope with her displeasure, although if such a thing should happen, rest assured it would give the rest of us a jolly good laugh."

Steven started to turn a shade of crimson, a mixture of embarrassment and anger.

"Fuck you, Fenston!" he roared, his temper finally reaching tipping point. Fenston raised his hands in mock surrender, his face tinged with a smirk.

"Now now, Steven, let's not get too excited, no need to throw the proverbial dummy out of the pram, you are an adult after all and as such you have some very special work to do this evening, don't you? We wouldn't want anything to happen that may jeopardise said work and cast you in a bad light, would we?"

Steven clenched his fist with the intention of lashing out but could feel hostile eyes at his back. He resisted the urge and when he slowly turned around, he was confronted by all of the bars other patrons, all of which were on their feet glaring at him. Each person clasped a glass bottle as if ready to engage in violence upon receiving the command from their friendly barman. He relaxed his grip, knowing full well he was out of his depth and that any confrontation would inevitably lead to him failing his first test. He smiled at the baying crowd and returned his attention to the smug and leering instigator behind the bar.

"Hah, well, well, this is a turn out for the books. A little over dramatic and somewhat unnecessary but believe it or not I would have to agree with that assessment, I'm sure Mistress has big plans for me, and it wouldn't be worth the risk. Having said that, it would appear I am no longer welcome at The Horny Toad, or am I mistaken? And now that you mention it, what do you know about any job I may or may not have to do? I'm pretty sure there would be no need for you to require such information. Could it be possible that you are not as well regarded as you once thought?"

Fenston gestured the room with his hands, undisturbed by the younger man's quip.

"Well, Sir, that is entirely down to you, isn't it? It appears you have a choice: you can either be a good boy and play by the rules or face the consequences of your perilous actions. What will it be, Steven? With regards to your imminent and, some might say, exciting job, may I suggest you be on your way and purchase the necessary tools on which your mission so obviously depends? I do believe the hardware store around the corner is open for business and would be happy to assist. And by the by, rest assured that Mistress holds me in higher regard than any other and you would do well to remember that."

Steven swallowed hard. How the fuck did Fenston know about the task given? He feigned acknowledgement, not wanting to play into the barman's obvious trap or engage in a pointless battle of wits.

Bide your time and keep cool. His time will come.

"I have no idea what you are talking about."

"Of course not, Sir. I do apologise if my words and actions have appeared out of turn. Let's finish our drinks and forget about such petty squabbles. We are both of the same ilk, you and I, and as such should stick together and support one another, would you not agree?"

Steven nodded, eager to diffuse the escalating disagreement and raised his glass to his mouth. He suddenly stopped as something caught his eye. He could have sworn he had just seen movement, movement within the amber liquid poised at his lips. He held the glass higher to gain a better look and couldn't believe what he saw. Within the glass he could see four or five black shapes gently swimming back and forth, each with a bulbous head and long tapering tail. Their bodies were a slick looking shiny black and they were all approximately four centimetres in length. He strained closer and could see they had tiny white eyes just above what looked like mouths. He sucked in a deep breath when one opened revealing a vicious looking set of teeth. It grinned at him maliciously then closed it again and continued on its way. Steven put down the glass and glanced at the barman, wondering if he was aware of his confusion and shock at the sinister looking creatures.

The older man remained silent, staring blankly at his customer. Steven reached down to retrieve his coat and got to his feet ready to leave. Fenston looked at his unfinished drink then raised his gaze to Steven.

"What's the hurry, Sir, don't you wish to finish your drink before you depart? I'm sure your "important" job will be thirsty work, and we all know that we must always remain hydrated when taking part in any form of strenuous exercise."

"No, that's ok, Fenston. I think it's time I should be heading home, lots to do and all that. I might pop in tomorrow if you are open." He slipped on his jacket and zipped it up, a sudden chill biting at his skin.

"No problem, Steven, in that case I shall bid you a fond farewell and wish you safe travel. I'm sure we will be seeing you again soon. Enjoy your evening."

Steven half-heartedly smiled by way of reply and made his way to the door all the while cautiously eyeing the other patrons, all of which were sat silently staring at him as he exited the building.

Once he had left and they were sure he was out of ear shot the room erupted into raucous laughter, every customer began shaking hands and high fiving each other, their sudden cheery mood infectious. Fenston too was laughing, tears of joy streaming down his face, his sides aching from exertion. He raised his hands to silence the revelry.

"Ok, Ok friends, just simmer down." the room hushed giving way to eager ears. "I know you are all excited and overjoyed regarding current events, but we aren't out of the woods just yet. Let's all keep our fingers crossed that Steven does what he's told and doesn't fuck it up. Only a few more days and we can sit back and finally relax but until then, we all have to play it cool; the Mistress demands it, ok?"

The room was filled with another resounding cheer agreeing with the statement then silence followed once again as the patrons returned to their own private conversations. Fenston was still smiling as he returned to wiping down the bar. "Not long now," he muttered under his breath.

Eight

Despite the slight chill in the air, Steven was feeling unnaturally warm, his new-found sense of bravado boldly announcing that it was due to the growing excitement regarding his imminent actions. But in truth, it was probably due to the fact that he was scared. Not scared of being caught, scared of cataclysmic failure in the eyes of his Mistress. All he could do was attempt to calm his nerves and get the job done as efficiently as possible. Fortune favours the brave he repeatedly told himself, an internal mantra to sooth his clawing negativity and thoughts of pending and possible inadequacy.

After leaving the bar he had gone directly to the hardware store, and with cash, purchased two non-descript hammers and a handful of other useless items so as not to raise any suspicion. The shop worker had barely made eye contact with him, let alone taking the time to scrutinize the contents of his basket. He had then decided it prudent to walk to the church and do a general sweep of the area should anything go wrong. He had seen countless movies and indulged in enough computer games to know that you should always do a "Recce" when embarking on a dangerous mission. He wasn't too sure what the term meant, in any case, at the very least he could make plans for his escape route, should things take a turn for the worst. As like any good soldier who uses the environment to his advantage, he even put aside his general dislike for rain and embraced the gradually deteriorating weather. The increasingly heavy downpours shielded his actions from any intrusive or nosey spectators who might let their eyes linger upon him for too long.

St Benedict's Church itself was situated just off the same high street that the bar, and his place of work were on. It's high, grime laden blackened steeple a visual signpost for those who became lost in the maze of side roads surrounding it. In truth, Steven had never paid it much attention. He had never been religious and even if he had been it certainly wouldn't be Christianity, ergo, he wasn't really interested. But now of course he had little choice, and quite frankly couldn't wait to get inside and get started, the prize offered being worth any snippet of discomfort in the short term.

The walk from the bar to his current location had been brief and non-descript however, it had afforded him the time to truly mull things over and really probe the events he now found himself part of. Steven couldn't believe the transformation he had undergone in only a matter of days. In such a short space of time, he had metamorphosed from some meek and timid nobody, into an apex predator free from the constraints of modern society and its superficial whims. All thanks to something as insignificant as visiting a bar. Of course, the real reason for his sudden change was the Mistress and the freedom she had offered, a key of sorts, to unlock his true potential and give meaning to his existence. The one thing that was gnawing at him was Fenston's sudden deteriorating attitude and, in all honesty, his now apparent disdain for him had caught Steven on the back foot. He surmised that it was down to good old-fashioned jealousy and, to be honest, with good reason. Steven felt as if he had been elevated to a lofty position, entrusted with an errand of paramount importance. Obviously, he didn't fully comprehend to what end, but all that mattered was the fact that the Mistress had chosen him over the rest. It stood to reason that others would view this as a slight against them personally, and their loyalty. Inevitably they would vent their frustrations at the only thing they could get away with without fear of reprisals, in this case, Steven.

The novice killer tugged back his heavy coat sleeve and inspected his watch. 18:30 hrs. Nearly time to get going. He had been sitting on a bench within the small church garden for most of the day, his actions disguised by drinking numerous cups of takeaway coffee and reading a book. He didn't think anyone would pay him a second glance if they believed him to be some stressed out office worker enjoying a well-deserved day off, or a broken man seeking solace and comfort in the grounds of a holy sanctuary. However serene his surroundings, he couldn't help but notice that the garden was embarrassingly overgrown and somewhat unkempt. Not that it had any bearing on his current mission, but one would have thought that with the amount of money the church had in its possession, and its immeasurable resources, they would be able to keep on top of it. Judging by his current location, it would appear the funds had been syphoned into other, more pressing requirements.

Steven chuckled as he remembered the old joke "If money is the route of all evil, why do they ask for it in church?" It would seem that no one had the answer to that particular question, or at least one the church would admit too. Funny what the mind thinks of when facing times of uncertainty and stress.

The fact it was raining harder now had somewhat negated his plan and he had since sought refuge under a rather substantial oak tree. As it happened, it had a perfect line of sight to the church narthex. For the past half hour, Steven had witnessed ten people enter the dirt encrusted stone building and couldn't help but think that they had no idea what lay instore for them once huddled inside. The delusion of their god giving them sanctuary was almost laughable. He reached his hand inside his jacket and for the sixth time, let his fingers touch the hardened metal heads of the hammers hidden within. The smooth, cold texture giving reassurance and peace of mind. He smiled and got to his feet. After readjusting his jacket, he gave the area one last survey then, when satisfied, began heading towards the entrance to the church.

If the outside appearance gave the impression of a dire lack of funding, the interior gave the complete opposite. Upon entering, Steven could smell the aroma of scented candles and wood polish, the well-worn stone flagged floor well maintained and fresh looking despite its age and regardless of the weather outside. The impressive stain glass windows cast multi coloured rainbows across saintly iconography and prized silver wear, adding to the impressive interior. Steven closed the heavy wooden door, the clunk echoing off the building's walls and vaulted ceiling. He paused to let the sound subside and began to study the rows of pews neatly arranged before him, deciding where best to place himself. He reasoned that the most logical place should be at the back as to be able to get to, then somehow lock or barricade the door, thus stopping people from escaping and alerting the authorities. All he had to do then was make his way forward lashing out at anything that came within striking distance. Chances were the vicar would be the first to die as he would no doubt feel the need to approach and attempt to talk him down whilst his parishioners backed away seeking salvation. This, of course, would have little effect on the inevitable outcome, as he would get to them soon enough. That being said, even best laid plans can go awry and if that should happen, the worst-case scenario was that a few may flee in the confusion and escape via some other unknown exit. As long as he got as many as he could he would have been, in his eyes, successful.

He eyed the handful of people already seated, their positions scattered and dispersed. All of them appeared to be on their own save one couple at the very front, their arms entwined around each other's shoulders, their heads resting together. He was surprised that none had turned to investigate his intrusion. Most likely lost in their own thoughts, begging their god to fulfil their wishes or respond to their prayers. He couldn't help but feel sorry for them, not for the fact that he was about to send them to their maker, but for believing that their "God" actually gave a shit in the first place. He silently surveyed each potential victim one last time, all of them sat motionless, waiting patiently for the arrival of their saintly shepherd.

He moved forward and sat himself two rows from the back, the chances of anyone sitting behind him were highly unlikely, especially as it was nearly time for the service to begin. Suddenly a bang alerted him to another's arrival. He turned to face the late addition and was relieved to see a frail looking old lady dressed in a bright purple dress and matching hat, her handbag clutched in one hand, a walking stick in the other. She ambled forward and slowly lowered herself on the first pew by the door directly behind him. She nodded a subdued greeting but remained silent. He looked on as she rummaged in her handbag, retrieved a handkerchief then placed her belongings beside her on the wooden bench. He gave the briefest of smiles and returned his attention to the front, not wanting to give the old lady an excuse to engage in conversation. If it had been some other, more able-bodied person, it would have undoubtedly bothered him and may very well have posed a problem. After checking her out, he was more than confident that once he stood and instigated his plan, he would be able to get to the door before she even realised what was happening, let alone put up any resistance. Oh well, looks like she is first on the list. Silly old cow shouldn't have sat there.

The abrupt commotion at the front of the church made Steven align his attention. He felt his body tense as he watched the hunched and shuffling figure of the vicar appear from the vestry door and take his position at the pulpit. He bade welcome to his flock and began the service. Steven couldn't help but notice his scrawny frame and balding head, wisps of white hair combed over to one side to disguise the rapid follicle demise, his features pinched and hawk-like. He glanced at his watch. 19:00 hrs. Dead on time. The vicar may have been odd looking and somewhat spiritually delusional but at least he was punctual. The frail and elderly looking clergyman cleared his throat, the phlegmy coughing exuberated by the vastness of the church's interior.

"Good evening everybody, please accept my apologies, I'm feeling a tad under the weather this evening. Thank you all for coming. I had hoped that more of you would have been in attendance, but as I look around I am confident that this should suffice. I trust that all of you are well and in fine spirits and that our lord and saviour has blessed you and your families with humility of heart and good health since the last time we met."

There was a muffled response from the sparse congregation. Steven stifled a snigger at the lack of religious enthusiasm and found himself willing the vicar to shut up and get on with it, failing that, save him the hassle of chasing him and just drop dead.

"Of course, despite the love of Jesus in our souls, we all have our ups and downs. Its part and parcel of life, and sometimes we may lose our way spiritually but regardless of the many bumps in the road, or the burdens of modern living that are sent to test us, we find the strength to keep fighting. Those of you who have found the courage to come this evening are most humbly welcome and without doubt, will be rewarded with the greatest of gifts. Some of you may be lost while others may be in denial, but I am certain that ninety nine percent of us know why we are truly here. Not only to give thanks to our lord and saviour …" he raised his gnarled and hairless head and glared towards the back of the church, "… but to rain down unholy carnage and unleash hellfire unto that useless and spineless piece of human shit, Steven, who you may notice is sitting at the back of this very church with plans of murdering us all."

The vicar suddenly threw his head back, his neck snapping with the force of the abrupt and jarring movement. He let out a mournful scream then slumped forward over the lectern, his body beginning to shake violently, his facial features expanding and contracting as if his skin was possessed of a fluid state. Thick, dark red blood began to seep from his eyes and ears, a trickle at first but soon a violent and inhuman deluge, the liquid not only spraying the highly polished woodwork but gathering in ever increasing pools around him. He spoke again but this time the voice was distorted, an abhorrent mix of growl and cognitive speech. It was as if his vocal chords and throat had been flooded with caustic acid. Steven looked on as he raised his arm, gently extended his finger and pointed directly at him.

"I would now like to invite the congregation to feast upon his entrails."

Steven froze, his entire body pulsing from the sudden adrenalin dump. He feverishly scanned the room and at the ten faces now glaring at him, their eyes cold and hostile. In unison they rose to their feet, their movements awkward, their limbs twisting and snapping out of alignment. Amid the chaos, Steven's ears began to be filled with the muted sounds of severed flesh and the ripping of limbs. Terrified, he watched on helplessly as savage serpent like tendrils began to emerge from his pursuer's faces and torsos, their clothes violently torn from their rapidly changing bodies by the force of the extrusions.

The violent and enraged cries of horror galvanised him into action. He leapt to his feet and threw himself to one side, desperate to get to the centre of the isle. The fear of becoming trapped between the rows of narrow seating sending shock waves around his body, but as he powered forward, his foot caught the leg of the pew in front causing him to lose balance. With arms flailing he tumbled forward, the momentum of which sent him crashing to the floor. He reached out in a desperate attempt to slow his decent, but it was of little use and with a dull thud, Steven's head collided with the stone slab. Everything around him suddenly went black, his vision blinded by the mix of the impact and the blood seeping from a newly opened wound above his left socket. In a state of confusion and disarray, he managed to scramble to his feet and rubbed his eyes on his sleeve, determined to regain the use of his most valuable sense. All around him the air was a cacophony of bestial guttural moans, the atmosphere savage and primordial, the stench of decrepitude clawing at the very fabric of his reality. He dragged himself upright, his momentary lack of balance causing him to rock violently from side to side, his body weight very nearly causing him to once again fall to the ground. With one hand, he reached out and grabbed hold of the wooden seat to steady his movement, and with the other, he blindly lashed out with a vicious punch, his survival instinct desperate to protect his body from the inevitable assault. He threw another, then almost cried tears of joy as his vision returned, cloudy and nebulous at first but back to normal within a matter of seconds. He let out a lungful of air, his relief almost palpable when he saw his tormentors were still in the same positions as before. His relief was but a moment of hope as the realisation slammed home that they were, in fact, toying with him and had remained stationary as per command.

It was then that Steven looked about him and couldn't find the words to describe what he was witnessing. On every wall, and even the ceiling, monstrously large black rips began to materialise, each one appearing to weave in and out of the very masonry and architecture. Their movements delicate and beautiful yet so obviously born of desolation and despair, for nothing so heinous could be born in such a holy place. As the rifts grew in size, Steven could do nothing more than stand transfixed by the ethereal dance playing out around him, his reason all but lost to a whirlwind of insanity. Like a growing crescendo, strange sounds began to emanate from the growing darkness that reverberated around the building's cavernous interior. The sound of distant wailing could be heard as well as, what Steven imagined, were the spectral sounds of the furthest reaches of space itself, the tones cold, harsh and abrasive. He looked on in a mixture of awe and consternation, his body numb with the growing feeling that unseen things were beginning to take an interest and were stirring from their slumber, for within each tear, unspeakable things began to turn their attention towards him. They seemed eager to either welcome the stranger into their personal oblivion, or feast upon this new and enticing world so pleasingly offered to them without fight nor recourse. Regardless of his fear, Steven's body refused to move, his limbs unresponsive to his desire to flee. All he could do was look on in terror as the ancient ones began to slowly reveal themselves from the blackened void. As the discordant drone increased in volume, a multitude of chaotic serpent like creatures began to push forward, eager to be released from their starless aeon, the need to remain hidden all but forgotten. The young assassin swallowed hard as he realised there was nothing he could do. The overbearing feelings of utter powerlessness and insignificance pulsing around his body as the creatures tentatively entered the light. Colossal tentacles slowly exited the rifts and began probing the building about them. Their tips flicked at obstructions, their vicious looking barbs sought a new form of sustenance. Steven cautiously eyed the creature's explorative extremities silently praying they would leave him be. Their bodies were shiny, the colour a mixture of dark green and mottled black, all of which contained what looked like a hundred eye balls curiously taking in the world around them. Steven remained motionless, his body immobilised by fear and a sudden noticeable drop in temperature. He held his breath as the hideous tentacles glided silently past him, their movements elegant yet unmistakably predatory. He watched on as emotionless eyes scrutinised him as they passed, the distance close enough to clearly see the pupils, they were obsidian and devoid of empathy yet self-aware and alert. He lowered his head, his gaze resting on the congregation who now stood motionless, their own heads raised to the heavens, their posture as if in silent worship to the unholy creatures entering this world.

Steven caught the vicar's stare, his facial expressions couldn't fail to alert the clergyman to his own bewilderment, his mind free falling under the watchful eyes of the ancient ones purposely stalking all around him. He watched on as the vicar grinned, his mouth a show of monstrously large and jagged teeth. Try as he might, Steven couldn't break his gaze as the former holy man stooped forward, his elongated fingers clutching at the pulpit, his nails carving large gouges into the wooden iconography. The creature lowered its head and eyed its parishioners malevolently then nodded slowly, his subordinates instantly knowing what the signal implied.

As if hunting as a pack, the ten figures locked their eyes upon Steven and began their advance towards him. Throaty and discordant sounds of gargled agony emanated from their mouths, behind them, the lashing of tentacles and barbs adding to the surreal symphony. Steven took a step back and with trembling fingers quickly unzipped his jacket uncovering his hammers. He took one in each hand and tightened his grip, his knuckles turning white from the pressure. He scanned the chaos around him, adjusted his stance and gawked at the approaching abhorrence. He stood his ground, and with his courage near to breaking point, prepared to be attacked.

Nine

Steven hurriedly used his sleeve to wipe blood and sweat from his brow and braced himself for the inevitable bloodbath. But just as he was about to press forward, something gave him pause, his sixth sense warning him of some unseen, yet imminent threat. It was at that moment he heard the deep clunking sound to his rear. He threw a quick glance over his shoulder just in time to see the purple dressed old lady locking the heavy wooden door with an iron key. Steven eyed her in disbelief as she tossed it to one side and turned to face him, he gasped at the sight of what was left of her face grinning maniacally, her teeth rotting and decayed.

"What the fuck?" he muttered under his breath as her discoloured and repugnant looking flesh began to droop uselessly from her neck and head in thick lumps, allowing an abundance of thin white tendrils to emerge unhindered. Their parasitical bodies reached out as if to taste the very air and sniff out their prey. Steven watched on as her body began to shake violently, her movements erratic and wild. Without warning she reached over with her left hand, and in one vicious movement ripped off her right arm and discarded it to the floor. Its fingers still moved as if possessed of sentient consciousness and desperate to re-join the fracas. Steven looked on in horror as her exposed shoulder muscles and ravaged flesh began to pulse rhythmically, then were abruptly torn asunder as three monstrous looking tentacles burst forth from the gaping shoulder wound and began to lash about in a frenzy. The old lady paused, threw her head back, and with a sepulchral scream, charged forward. Her arm and hell-spawned appendages raised and ready to tear into her intended victim.

For a split-second, and in the face of the truly absurd, Steven began to panic. He shuffled backwards and immediately stumbled to one side but as he did so, on instinct, pulled back his right arm and with eyes closed, and all his strength propelled it forward. There was a deafening crack as the old lady ran forward into the full force of the arc of the hammer, her distorted hungry mouth mere inches from Steven's face, the tendrils desperately lashing out at his flesh, her appendages whipping about his body. Steven couldn't help but grin in triumph as the left side of her head caved in under the heavy blow, the force of the impact sending her sprawling to the floor. The young man regained his footing and remained vigilant as his attacker rolled onto her side and let out an unholy shrill, the archaic sound reverberating around the church. Steven began to shake uncontrollably, the after effects of the colossal endorphin dump thumping in his temples. He cautiously stepped forward, his weapons primed and ready to dish out other catastrophic blows upon the stricken abhorrence. He was confident he had done enough to finish it, but to Steven's astonishment, she managed to leap to her feet, once again throwing herself back at him. Surprised by the second attack Steven had little choice but to back off, but as he did so, his limbs went cold as he suddenly remembered the horrors advancing behind him.

He spun around just as a second creature launched itself at him, its clawed hands outstretched and demanding blood. In a state of blind panic Steven let loose another heavy right swing that once again hit its mark. The creature let out a discordant cry of agony as the force of the blow sent it flying through the air and crashing into the pews, its hefty body weight causing the wood to splinter and snap, the shards scattering the floor. Cautiously, Steven took a step forward, his adrenaline giving urgency to the need to finish it off with a death blow before it could regain its senses and come back at him. He struggled to catch his breath, his muscles and lungs aching from the constant battle fatigue and crushing sensations of perpetual fear. He leant over the upturned wooden bench and glared at the creature on the floor beneath him.

"Fuck you!" he bellowed as he raised his right hand then, with sickening speed, slammed the hammer down into the wounded creature's forehead. The abomination howled one final time as the heavy metal lump effortlessly carved its way into its brain sending a geyser of blood into the air, splashing both Steven and the area around him. The bloodied young man rose to his feet but didn't have time to revel in his victory. He let out a gargled scream as he suddenly felt savage finger nails rake at his back. He winced as he felt a wave of blood erupt from the wounds and cascade down his body, seeping into his already sodden clothes. Even without inspection or medical training he knew, in all probability, that he was seriously injured and that it was only a matter of time before he passed out from blood loss. With all the will and training in the world there was no way he could last much longer against the ever-increasing horde coming for him. Yet despite the insanity and with his body near to the point of complete exhaustion, his brain refused to submit. With an explosive howl of rage and defiance, he spun on his heels and lashed out with both hammers. His blows akin to absolute desperation as opposed to surgical or well-placed strikes. Even as the unspeakable terror relentlessly ripped and clawed at him, he kept flailing, his muscles burning from the intensity and ferocity of his movements. Blow after blow rained down on the otherworldly horror before him, the joyous sounds of flesh being pulverised and reduced to nothing more than liquid spurring him on, his indomitable will to survive fuelling his rapidly diminishing humanity. The choice before him was simple: fight or die, and unlike the Steven of old, he was now resolute to the fact that if he was going down, he would damn well make sure he wouldn't go without one hell of a fight!

Steven became aware that the creature had stopped moving and gradually slowed his attack, his body shaking from rage and exhaustion. He stared at the gore infused abomination lying at his feet, its chest rising and falling all but slightly, its now useless tentacles strewn across the wooden pew and stone flagging. Steven triumphantly stepped forward, raised his leg then with a final burst of power brought it down hard. His boot slammed into the creature's head, the impact sending a wave of blood and what looked like dark green puss in a wide arc from the body. He quickly shifted his attention between the carcass and the expanding puddle of repulsive fluids. His stomach lurched as the stench of rotting meat wafted around him, his immersion in pungent acrid air causing him to gag. Despite his best attempts to hold it back he couldn't help but vomit, the bile adding to the noxious melee splashed across wood, stone and twisted flesh. Steven rubbed his face with one hand, his gore encrusted weapons held tightly in the other.

What the hell was going on? He found himself repeating. This wasn't supposed to happen he told himself.

The air inside the church was suddenly filled with a mix of bestial howls and high pitched shrills. Steven turned, and once again had little choice but to face the advancing horde, his body near complete collapse both physically and emotionally. He surveyed the scene and counted five nearly upon him, their movements slower than before, more deliberate yet just as menacing. He took in a short intake of breath as he identified the nearest foe. It was the vicar himself, his robes bloodied and torn, his face practically unrecognisable. The creature paused, raised its head and cocked it to one side. Steven once again gripped his hammers, the anticipation of attack near breaking point. He kept watch as the creatures began to surround him in a loose semi-circle, the remainder of his foe hanging back behind the closest five.

"Come on, you bastards!" he rasped, eager to break the stalemate.

"What the hell are you waiting for!"

Just as he asked the question, there was a deafening crack of thunder from above, the detonation of which caused the very building to shake. Steven instinctively ducked to protect himself from the deluge as large chunks of masonry were dislodged from the ceiling and sent tumbling to the floor. The creatures howled as clouds of dust were whipped up around them, their cries adding to this new scene of cosmic chaos. He gritted his teeth and clenched his eyes tight, the audio onslaught almost too much to bare but despite his passive and crouched position. He could sense movement from above and knew if he was to escape with his life, he had little choice but to investigate. Slowly and cautiously, he once again rose to his feet and through the wafts of dust and grime, forced his eyes to gaze up to the heavens. In the face of infinite horror, he held his breath at the sight of yet more gargantuan tentacles appearing from the void. But this time there was something else, something that caused Steven to sink into even deeper realms of despair, the new feeling negating any previous sense of terror yet presented. Above him from the midst of the tears, were eight huge eyes, each the size of a small van and all of which were staring down directly at him. Steven stared back, his eyes welling with tears, his will to fight almost vanquished completely by the monstrosities before him.

"What the fuck do you want from me?" he sobbed.

As if answering his plea, the building was rocked by another deafening crack of thunder and a furious lashing of tentacles against the surrounding structure, the impact of which sent yet more debris crashing to the floor. Steven looked on through bloodshot and myopic eyes as the giant stain glass window suddenly imploded, the force sending a wave of tiny glass projectiles in all directions. He turned his body slightly but unlike before, he remained on his feet, his refusal to submit and cower on the ground surprising even himself.

Amongst the maelstrom, Steven suddenly noticed movement out of the corner of his eye, he turned to see the former vicar's body begin to shake, its grotesque head bobbing and rolling from side to side. Steven tensed, gripped his hammers and prepared for another attack but as he did so, he began to hear faint muffled noises emanating from its mouth, he cocked his ear, and started to doubt his senses, for he could swear that the creature was trying to laugh, the noise garbled and throaty at first but then increasing in volume and intensity. Steven couldn't believe what he was hearing. He watched on in a state of chronic denial as every single one of the creatures began to laugh hysterically, as if taking the vicars lead, human sounds of merriment and amusement corrupted by bestial and demonic blights. The monster killer glanced over his shoulder towards the iron key lying on the ground towards the front of the church then to the heavy door itself. Could he make it before the creatures got to him?

Without thinking, he powered forward, his legs forcing his torso to move and catch up. Behind him the laughter turned to howls of rage as his tormentors realised his intentions. Steven dared not look back but could hear the creatures giving chase, their bodies barging fallen wreckage from their path as they accelerated towards him. He increased his speed and charged towards the iron key lying on the floor. He reached out his hand and snatched up his prize then sprinted for the doorway, his heart pulsing from the sudden adrenaline dump. With the door within reach, he extended his arm and slid the key into the lock and twisted. Just as he heard the mechanism disengage, a massive blow from behind caused him to slam forward face first into the door. Steven tried to hold on to his senses, the brutality of the impact causing his head to swim violently and his vision to blur. Fearing a secondary attack, he managed to drop his body weight and turned just in time to dodge a tentacled barb firing forward. He held his breath as it hammered past his face, narrowly missing his eyeballs and imbedded itself into the wood. He turned and winced as an explosion of tiny splinters showered his face, biting at his already bloodied and bruised skin.

There was an ear-piercing wail as the creature tugged at its ensnared body part then howled in rage as it retracted its weapon and prepared to launch another assault. As it charged forward Steven tried to stand but his legs gave way from under him, the muscles fatigued and unresponsive. He let out a mournful groan as his body crashed to the floor with a heavy thump. Once again, he scrambled to get to his feet, the creature before him gaining ground and now just metres away, its organic weapons raised and ready to be unleashed once again.

Amidst the confusion, Steven lost his grip on his hammers, the slick and blooded handles sliding from his grasp. He grimaced and felt his stomach drop as he saw them tumble from his hands and skid across the floor out of reach. As if knowing its victim was defenceless, the creature lashed out with three tentacles, the tips of which slithered and wrapped around Steven's left leg and began to drag him towards its gaping mouth, its teeth eager to taste and savour the young man's flesh. Steven reached out, desperate to find something to defend himself with. His hands grasping and clawing amid the rubble strewn about him. As the appendages pulled him closer, Steven felt something touch his hand, he glanced towards the object and immediately snatched it up, his grip firm and well placed. He returned his gaze to his relentless tormentor, and with its hungry mouth just inches away, threw his right hand forward, his makeshift weapon his last line of defence.

Stuart R Brogan

Ten

With a scream of defiance Steven gripped his weapon as tight as possible and rammed the thick wooden shard into the roof of the creature's mouth. It reared backwards, its tentacles momentarily releasing him from their grip. The young warrior realised what was happening and took advantage of the chance offered. He held on, and with a final burst of power, thrust the sharp point further through its thick jaw muscles and into the soft welcoming tissue of its brain; the tip puncturing the apex of the cranium and out through the top of its head. There was an unholy chorus of reticent moans as the abomination spasmed and fell to its knees, its body flailing, blood gushing from its eyes, mouth and other extremities. Steven grinned at the sight of the horror sucking in its final breaths and once again pushed the stave even deeper. His hands ached from the pressure, his temples throbbing from the exertion. He still had hold of his weapon when, with a raspy intake of breath, the monstrosity slumped forward and landed dead on the floor. Its brains leaked from the gaping wound in its mouth and from the hole in the top of its skull.

Steven's momentary respite was shattered by the discordant wail of the dead creature's brethren hurtling towards him, their bodies a whirling mass of teeth and tentacles, their audible screeches growing in ferocity. He glanced upwards, above him the colossal beasts stirred and squirmed as if agitated and angered by the loss of one of their own, their movements fluid and graceful. He quickly turned and ferociously tugged open the heavy door, the sudden movement threatening to tear it from its hinges. He lunged forward and ran from the building as fast as his legs would allow, his desire to face more horrors all but a distant memory. He powered harder, his body overcome with exhaustion yet somehow knowing the importance of keeping the pace going and understanding the consequences should it falter. As he sucked in huge lungsful of frosty cold air, he kept his focus on the direction of travel and not once did he dare look back over his shoulder, his curiosity for explanations secondary to his need for escape and survival. He raced through the overgrown and shadow-swept graveyard, through the rusting cast iron gates, and accelerated down the side street towards the main road. Behind him he could hear terrible things give chase, the crunch of gravel, the scuffs of wet flesh upon tarmac, the otherwise tranquil night a cacophony of cosmic hatred closing in around him. High above him, dark and sinister clouds seemed to swirl and dance. The moon itself was covered by a thick blanket of what looked like mist, yet it was unlike any he had witnessed before; its viscosity otherworldly. He kept moving, his muscles burning, begging for respite. Even when he reached the deserted and deathly quiet main road, he did not give pause. Past abandoned cars, their engines still running, their doors wide open. Past empty shops, their colourful displays still illuminated and alluring. None posed distraction or held interest, his only desire to reach his home safely, to barricade his doors and windows and seek refuge from the terrors being unleashed upon humanity.

Steven did not see one solitary person on his journey, nor any signs of human activity. The streets around him devoid of life and late-night revelry, splattering of blood and unrecognisable pools of gore the only indication of anyone ever being present. In the face of the chaos he pushed on, his senses forced to attune to the growing darkness enveloping his urban surroundings. For some reason, everything appeared to be a lot more sinister. The atmosphere appeared malignant and was growing ever more oppressive with every passing moment. The most innocuous and trivial of things now seemed haunting and dangerous. As he kept a steady pace he would give more than cursory glances towards blackened doorways and the darkest of recesses. Every now and then he would catch fleeting signs of movement from the corner of his eye. He would tremble as he caught sight of hunched, black figures skulking amongst the shadows, their body mechanics giving the impression of neither man nor animal but something else entirely. Sometimes, all he would see was the glint of street lamps dancing upon the white orbs of hellish transgressions, their attentive stare watching his every move yet remaining hidden.

Steven hadn't heard anything behind him for some time, and it was possible that his pursuers had given up the chase. It was more likely that they had become less overt in their endeavours, favouring stealth over a blatant and obvious frontal attack. Regardless of his lack of social status and what others would argue back in the real world, Steven knew that he possessed some degree of intelligence and wasn't in fact as stupid as others would believe. As such, he didn't want to take any unnecessary risks, for his instinct was telling him that they were indeed still out there, in the gnawing gloom, stalking and hunting him.

It would appear, that they were playing with him, for any number of beasts could have finished him off whilst he travelled his lonesome journey. Regardless of recent events Steven couldn't get the image of the Mistress from his mind. Her long black hair, her piercing eyes. The truth was that he longed for her even more than ever before; longed to worship at the altar of flesh. It stood to reason that Fenston was behind the circumstances of his catastrophic failure and the architect of unspeakable horrors. Steven decided to cut all ties with the barman, should he still be alive that is.

As Steven rounded a corner he smiled, a wave of relief washing over him. The imposing silhouette of his block of flats a welcoming sight upon his weary and bloodshot eyes. He paused to catch his breath and looked about him, the search for threats ever present and of paramount importance. When satisfied the coast was clear, he lowered himself into a crouch and cautiously manoeuvred himself between abandoned cars and entered the tenements main entrance. He was extremely relieved to be back on familiar territory and the safety of his fifth-floor abode.

Steven burst through his front door and slammed it shut behind him. He quickly fastened the deadbolt and grabbed a wooden chair from his kitchen. He returned quickly and wedged it against the handle, he knocked the chair with his hand and was happy to see that it was sturdy. He let out a sigh of relief. The makeshift barricade wasn't infallible, but as a temporary measure it would have to do. He darted to the windows in every room and quickly drew the curtains, desperate to keep whatever lurked outside far from the confines of his sanctuary. He retrieved his gore-encrusted hammers and tossed them on his kitchen table then threw his blood-soaked jacket into the bathroom. The clawing stench of iron was beginning to make him feel nauseous. Before he collapsed on his sofa, the last thing he retrieved was the biggest and most vicious looking kitchen knife he possessed. He placed the wickedly sharp blade on his small table and eyed the shiny metal. Regardless the size of the weapon, it gave him little reassurance considering the odds he faced, but beggars can't be choosers he thought. Once again, the seductive image of the Mistress abruptly appeared before him as if taunting his humanity and willing him to concede. Of course, to her he would give anything, but whilst those creatures hunted him, he had little choice but to hide.

He slumped into the soft embrace of the furniture and closed his eyes, desperate to grab some semblance of peace. He gently massaged his forehead and exhaled. His conscious mind struggling with what had befallen him and the actions thrust upon him. His mind raced with a hundred questions, the answers of which infuriatingly alluded him. Contradictory views thrashed it out, a whirlpool of emotions causing his rationale to second guess every thought pattern or reasoning.

What the fuck was happening? Why had the Mistress led him to such a place only to have him killed by those abominations?

The loud knock at the front door made Steven jump to his feet, his hand instinctively snatching up the blade and clasping it tight. He glared at the front door, his body poised for the aperture to be smashed open at any second, a wave of horror and snarling hatred no doubt moving swiftly behind it. With the noise of his heart ringing in his ears he moved slowly towards the entrance. His movements cautious and steady, his breathing low as to not alert whatever lay beyond to his presence. Step by step he edged closer, all the while listening for movement. The second loud knock made him freeze. He was only three feet from his barricade, he cursed under his breath because the main door didn't possess a peep hole. He couldn't see for himself what was responsible without physically opening the door. He glanced around the room, analysing possible escape routes should it be necessary to evacuate. Again, another loud and forceful knock, then subtle signs of movement from beyond. Steven strained his hearing as the soft sounds of nails scraping upon wood grew louder. Soft throaty growling began to resonate from the darkened hallway. Steven swallowed and gripped his blade even tighter.

"Come now Steven, we come not to do you harm, but to engage in civilised conversation."

The young man paused, stunned by the sudden and instantly recognisable voice.

"Fenston?" he croaked quietly.

There was a soft chuckle followed by an audible sigh.

"Indeed, my friend. I have come to sit, parley and break bread with one who I deem a friend. Are you not prepared to sit and speak with me a while? To offer a weary traveller a drink and a few moments of your time? Did I not offer you the same hospitality when you first visited my abode?"

Confused, Steven rubbed his eyes with his free hand, the beginnings of a headache stabbing at his frontal lobe. He stared at the door, unsure of how to proceed. Once again, his brain began to second guess any previous reasoning, there was simply no way of knowing if Fenston bore him any ill intent. Sure, the Mistress had led him into the church but was it possible that she was not responsible for what happened next? For the creatures so eager to enter our world and devour the flesh of those they encountered? How could she be, she was a Goddess after all! Steven was confident that the Mistress harboured no such nefarious intent, but Fenston on the other hand was…another story.

"How, how the hell are you still alive?"

There was a brief pause then Fenston spoke again, his tone cheerful.

"I know you have a lot of questions and I would be happy to answer them, let us move forward together and start afresh."

Steven glanced at his weapon then to the door, desperately trying to decide his course of action.

"Where the fuck is everybody? Have you any idea what I just saw, what's outside in the shadows?"

"Oh Steven, always one for needing explanations, the answers of which you couldn't possibly understand nor comprehend should they be presented. The fact of the matter is that the people of this fine city are not dead, nor are they technically alive, for you see they are merely becoming a higher form of evolution, a lifeform dedicated to the Mistress and her delectable ways."

Steven laughed out loud, his sudden retort catching even him by surprise.

"What the fucking hell are you on about, Fenston?"

"Come now, please be reasonable Steven, don't you think this conversation would be better suited face to face without this door between us? To have the opportunity to see the whites of each other's eyes, to gaze upon the cut of the other's jib? Why not let me in and we shall pop the kettle on and discuss things civilly, like proper gentlemen. What do you say? Do we have an accord?"

Steven had systematically weighed his options. He had little choice and he knew it. If he wanted answers, then letting Fenston in was the only way to get them. He may very well be giving his enemy the perfect opportunity to kill him but to be honest, his chances of survival on the street were next to zero. No matter which way you sliced it, he was fucked either way.

"Ok, hang on…" he mumbled begrudgingly, his decision made.

Steven reached down and removed the chair from under the latch and unlocked the bolt. He paused, his hand nervously hovering over the handle, the final security measure between himself and his would-be killer. He snatched at it and pulled open the door. He was greeted by the dapper looking barman dressed in a long black coat, his face beaming and holding out his hands.

"Now, isn't that better, Steven? It would appear we are making progress."

Steven cautiously took two steps back and gestured Fenston to enter. The new arrival nodded and moved forward, cautiously scanning the room as he did so, his eyes seeking out any possible threat. As Steven began to shut the door, he heard a low grumbling from the corridor. He turned to see two creatures move towards him from the darkness, their faces ripped and inhuman, their clothes nothing but bloodied rags hanging from corrupted and hellish bodies. He held his breath as they crawled silently past him and followed Fenston into the flat, their tentacles floating behind them as if suspended from above. Steven watched on as Fenston removed his coat and slumped down on the sofa, the creatures flanking him as if protecting him from nefarious intent. Steven closed the door and made his way tentatively to the living area, all the while keeping his gaze fixed on his enemy.

"Ok, you've got what you wanted, there's no longer a door between us. Say what you have got to say and leave, but it better be good or..." He glanced at the knife in his hand, then back to Fenston who had noticed the movement and understood completely, "...things are going to get messy."

As Steven's voice began to increase in volume, and in response to his threat, the two creatures edged forward, their claws extended and at the ready. Steven paused at the sight of them preparing to attack and slowly began to raise his blade. Fenston noticed the impending fracas and glared at his subordinates, smiled, then waved his hand dismissively. The creatures growled menacingly and backed away; visibly annoyed by their master's command. The bar tender let out a little chuckle.

"Don't worry young Sir. I fully comprehend your meaning and must apologise on behalf of my overzealous co-workers. They do so very much enjoy their work and are incredibly eager to show their loyalty at any given opportunity. Rest assured that it won't happen again, unless of course you try something silly."

Steven remained silent but kept his focus on the now motionless creatures, his weapon ready should he need it. He returned his attention to the older man.

"What the hell is happening Fenston? No more games. Are you responsible for all this?"

"My friend, that is such a deep and loaded question, with a multitude of answers, none of which you are going to like I'm afraid."

Steven could feel his temper rising, his grip instinctively applying more pressure on his knife handle.

"I say again, are you responsible for what happened to me in the church?" he growled menacingly.

Fenston shrugged.

"Would it make any difference if I said yes? Would it change your current predicament or save you from the atrocities that hunt outside these four walls? Would your chances of survival be increased if I admitted that I alone summoned the ancient ones from their slumber and set in place a sequence of events that would change everything? Did you not want to be present at the end of things and to witness the sun turn black?"

Steven sighed as he tried to keep his emotions in check, his rage towards Fenston was palpable. He moved to the kitchen, the need to be away from such self-righteousness over-powering, but all the while keeping tabs on his guests. He grabbed two bottles of water from the fridge as a pretext for a moment of respite then returned to the living space. He tossed one to Fenston, who caught it and nodded in gratitude.

"Where is the Mistress?" Steven asked, his tone subdued.

"Aaahhh, now we are getting down to the brass tacks, the nitty gritty of the issue at hand. It is my sad and embarrassing duty to inform you that she, is in fact, busy attending to other business. However, my dear friend, she has asked me to pass on her most sincere and heartfelt regards, and to also inform you of your second task."

"Second task? You're joking, right? With all that shit happening out there? Besides, I didn't even finish the first one, I was sure she would have been displeased with my performance."

"Not so Steven, for you see it was all pre-planned. Your task was to simply survive the encounter, and survive you did in spectacular style. You managed to face the ancient ones and live to tell the tale. I myself take my hat off to you, my intrepid young friend. Not many people have ever witnessed such archaic delights and walked away unscathed."

Steven took a swig from his water and wiped his parched lips on his jumper.

"So, she still wants me to be a part of her plan, to allow me to worship at the altar of flesh? Even though the church mission was a complete fuck up?"

Fenston got to his feet and extended his arms as if to welcome Steven into an embrace.

"Why of course! Why wouldn't she? You are so very crucial to her success, I'm sure you are smart enough to sense if something was amiss, and aware should you lose favour in the eyes of the Mistress. If you had, I dare say it would have become apparent before now. She doesn't really do subtle, if you know what I mean."

The young office worker relaxed his grip on the knife, his fears consoled by the explanation given. I was right, it was a test; the Mistress still values me.

"So then, what exactly is my second task? What could she possibly have me do when the whole world around us has gone to shit?" Fenston beamed again, his smile infectious, his humour somewhat enduring. "Why, isn't it obvious Steven…?"

Steven shrugged, his confusion evident.

"You have to stop me and my two associates from ripping you apart."

Stuart R Brogan

Eleven

Steven looked on in disbelief as Fenston's face began to undulate, slowly at first then with greater urgency. His rapidly darkening skin rippling and beginning to dangle from his muscle, cartilage and skull. The air was suddenly imbued with an unnatural and repugnant fleshy sound as his face began to tear apart in a vertical motion. The ordinarily fatal wound opened at his forehead, running down his nose, across his mouth and ending just below his chin. The changeling let out a cataclysmic shrill, its body writhing as if part of some macabre dance, the heavy mixture of ecstasy and agony fuelling its explosive decent into the most primitive and basic of desires.

Steven managed to turn his head just as a torrent of blood erupted from the former bar tenders head, splitting it in two. The ferocity of the transformation spraying the ceiling and the surrounding furniture. The younger man stumbled backwards, nearly tripping on his table but managed to keep himself upright. Unable to break his gaze, he stood in awe as the monstrous cavity gave way to four serpent-like tendrils emanating from where his throat had been mere seconds previous, each one dark green and savage looking, the length of which ran sinister looking hooks and barbs. Steven backed off even further for fear of being within striking distance and raised his blade in defiance.

He quickly scanned the room, willing an escape route to materialise, but nothing was forthcoming. He glanced at the front door then back to the scene of butchery before him. He felt his stomach lurch as Fenston's cheek muscles and fleshy ribbons hung discarded to the sides of his neck. They flapped uselessly as he suddenly lurched forward, his arms outstretched, his hands now transformed into claw like mandibles.

In the same moment, the other two creatures leapt into the air, their large, yet agile bodies easily vaulting the sofa between them and with a heavy thump, landed mere feet from where Steven was standing, their posture hunched and low. Then, without warning, and with incredible speed, one moved to Stevens left and circled the room. Steven sucked in a breath as he realised it was heading for the front door, no doubt its intention was to cut off his only escape route. The second remained stationary, its attention fixated solely on the young man who stood before it. It hissed menacingly and took a step towards him, its tentacles poised to flay flesh from bone.

Steven didn't waste any more time. He dropped his body weight and side stepped to his right and, using it as a shield from the main attacker, lunged forward, slamming the tip of the knife into the second creature's forehead. The creature violently reared as the young man retracted the blade and quickly struck again. From behind, the former bar tender pressed forward, desperate to get to its prey. It let out a scream of rage as its tentacles were unable to land a strike due to its subordinate being between it, and its quarry. Steven kept up the momentum and struck for a third time, the blade sinking up to the handle from the force of the trauma. He kept hold of the hilt and with both hands attempted to force the blade even deeper into the monstrosities' brain. The abomination howled in pain but instead of falling to its knees it suddenly lashed out with its tentacles which hit Steven squarely in the chest, the impact of which took him off his feet and sent him tumbling through the air. With an ear splintering smash of glass and wood Steven crashed into the TV unit, his upper torso slamming off the solid wall behind. His body crumpled and doubled over, his head slumping forward on his chest from the blunt force inflicted. He shook his head and tried to regain his senses, the urgency of his dire circumstances willing him to stand and fight. With his limbs shaking he reached out, his hands raking at the debris, desperately searching for his only weapon which had been dropped during the brutal attack.

As his faculties returned, his eyes fell upon his knife on the other side of the room, the blade out of reach and now well and truly out of use. The highly shined metal glinting seductively among the remnants of the decimated furniture. He shook his head once again and raised his eyes just as Fenston fell upon him, his claws latching securely around his throat, its nails piercing the skin and opening savage lacerations. Steven sucked in a shallow breath as he was forcibly dragged to his feet, his vision swimming from his rapidly diminishing oxygen supply. The horror let out a demonic shriek and tossed Steven effortlessly across the room and into the sofa, which toppled backwards, the momentum of which gave the young man no option but to go with it. Once again Steven slammed into the wall, the sudden and abrupt stop adding to his already diminished state of self-defence. Steven dragged himself to his feet and eyed the approaching monster, his body bloodied and bruised from the sustained and relentless attacks.

He wiped his eyes clear of blood and surveyed the room. The first creature was still positioned by the front door, unable or unwilling to join the fight. As Fenston gained ground, Steven looked past him, his attention drawn to the kitchen beyond. He smiled as the beginnings of a plan started to formulate in his mind. With a sudden surge of adrenaline, Steven threw himself over the sofa and managed to duck, just as Fenston lashed out. The younger man remained low as the creature's primary weapons sailed harmlessly above his head and crashed into the bookshelf, sending a deluge of ornaments and DVDs across the room. Steven pushed with his legs and almost toppled, his sudden loss of balance giving him momentary concern but using the momentum, he managed to get to his feet and once again found his stride. His focus on reaching the kitchen was his primary objective. Fenston screamed in rage and retracted his limbs then immediately turned and lunged forward, giving chase. His appendages flailed around his body as he moved, rasping sounds spewing forth from his gaping and hungry mouth that had appeared amongst the throng of tendrils, its teeth snapping with excitement.

Steven powered into the small kitchen and immediately reached for the cooker, his moist hands slipping on the slick metal knobs as he turned each of them up to the maximum setting. He sucked in a final deep breath as the confines of the kitchen began to fill with the noxious gas fumes belching freely from the appliance. He spun on his heels just as Fenston's now protruding mouth clamped down into his left shoulder, its rows of jagged teeth effortlessly carving their way through his jumper and into the flesh below. The younger man winced as more pressure was applied and let out a terrified scream as he felt the razor-sharp teeth hit bone. He tried to pull free, his arm now a torrent of blood gushing freely from the horrendous wound. With his right-hand Steven reached out, desperately trying to find some sort of weapon to aid his escape, all the while counting down the seconds before he would lose consciousness due to the unseen threat silently filling the room. Steven's hand briefly touched ceramic, he forced himself to turn and in a fit of desperation grabbed the dinner plate and smashed it on the work surface, leaving only a shard in his hand. He turned his body and thrust the shard into the side of Fenston's neck and with all his strength immediately began to drag the make shift blade towards his attacker's sternum. In a fit of torment Fenston momentarily released his grip allowing Steven to pull away, his left arm hanging uselessly by his side.

Fenston began to back off, the savage injury forcing him to halt his relentless advance. The young man pressed his advantage and snatched open one of the unit drawers, he pulled out a lighter then turned towards the still stumbling creature. The young man watched on as the former barman retreated into the living room. Steven slowly followed, the lighter and shard clutched in his right hand. The creature moved backwards, towards the front door and joined its unmoving subordinate, both eyed their pray as he diligently entered the room.

"Is this not a game of sublime and delectable joy?" Fenston croaked, his voice all but unrecognisable.

Steven swallowed hard, unsure how to respond to the faceless monster.

"I have no intensions of playing games."

Both creatures began to emanate a deep throaty chuckle, their limbs juddering.

Steven took a step, all the while keeping watch for any sudden movements. Then, with breath-taking speed, the second creature launched itself forward, leaving Fenston alone at the door. Steven's reflexes were too slow to react and before he could move out of the way, took the body blow from his attacker squarely in the stomach. In a swirly mass of bodies, both the young human and the clawing fiend tumbled backwards and into the kitchen once more. The smell of gas almost over bearing, the soft relentless hiss of its release ever present.

Steven lashed out with a closed fist, his left arm unable to assist in his defence. The creature managed to get to its feet first and began to rein vicious blows down upon its stricken quarry. Steven covered his head, his body taking the brunt of the punishing attack. Through blurry eyes he scanned the kitchen but couldn't see anything within easy reach. It was then he spotted the fire extinguisher in the corner of the room. He glanced up and waited for his moment.

Just as the horror recoiled its limbs, the beleaguered young man twisted his body, as if rolling over, and as he did so, forced his opponent to lose balance, topple to his right and slam head first into the cooker. Steven pushed off with his right hand and dragged himself to his feet. Behind him, it too regained its footing and turned to face him. Steven snatched up the red metal cylinder and glared at his advancing enemy. He wound up, then flinched slightly as he swung with every fibre of his being and smiled as the metal collided with the abomination's skull. The room instantly filled with the sound of cracking bone.

The creature staggered, momentarily dazed by the blow, its jaw hanging fruitlessly on its bloodied chest. Steven lunged forward and with one brutal yank, ripped the dangling body part free from the skull. In a gargling of blood and bile, the beast fell to the floor, its life force extinguished.

Steven sucked in a wheezing breath but instantly began to cough as the fumes attacked his lungs. He staggered from the kitchen, his head swimming from his prolonged exposure. As he entered the living room, he could see the former barman still present at the front door, its posture unflinching, its demeaner unconcerned with its prey's minor victory.

"Do you think you stand a chance against us, Steven?" it barked menacingly.

The young man paused by the large window and with his good shoulder struggled to nudge open the heavy curtains revealing the rotting glass and surround.

"Actions speak louder than words, Fenston, or whatever the fuck you are!"

He let out a mournful breath, there was no way out, he knew this was the end, everything had led to this moment. Oh, how he had wished that he had knelt at the altar of flesh, to be given the opportunity to prove his devotion, but thanks to Fenston he had been denied his desires. As he stood battered and bleeding before the beasts unleashed from the void, he strangely felt at peace. He glanced at the lighter, a slight wry smile touching the corner of his mouth. He nodded slowly, his last act of defiance in a world descending into oblivion he told himself. He glared at his assailant one last time and grinned as he engaged the lighter. The last thing Steven saw was the bright blue and orange flash as the gas filled room ignited.

A huge ball of fire erupted sending a pressure wave into every corner of the flat, the flames mercilessly clawing at, and devouring, everything that dared to stand in its way. The hells creation screamed in agony as the blast engulfed it, its body incinerating from the devastating heat and ensuing inferno.

Steven managed one last smile and closed his eyes, silently heeding his beckoning into the peaceful embrace of the next realm. He felt the sudden sensation of scorched flesh as the blast took him off his feet and blew him backwards through the window and out into the cold night air.

Stuart R Brogan

Twelve

The voice was delicate and distant at first, as if whispered in some desolate and cavernous room. A few seconds passed then it could be heard again, the same word repeated. An ethereal summoning to reawaken the shattered and beleaguered senses. A gentle nudge to reign in lost souls cast adrift upon starless oceans.

Try as he might, Steven couldn't see. He believed his eyes to be open but was surrounded by impenetrable darkness. He tried to focus, to find reason in his awakening, but no matter how hard he tried to find the answers, he knew deep down they wouldn't grant him any semblance of understanding. He heard the word again. Distant, yet getting closer. Somehow, he recognised it, as if some distant memory was being replayed to jolt him back to the present. He could do nothing else but answer its call.

"Yes, I'm here…" he whispered softly. "Where am I? am I dead?"

A gentle and subdued laugh emanated from the void around him, the resonance felt throughout his body, sending waves of ecstasy to the receptors in his brain.

"Who are you?"

There was a moment of silence followed by a chorus of voices, all of which appeared to be from the same being only at different pitches.

"Who do you believe me to be?" came the answer.

Steven swallowed and once again attempted to look about him, his body aching from the nothingness that gripped him so tightly.

"Are you the Mistress?"

He was embarrassed by his sickening lack of comprehension, for this was far beyond the limits of prescribed science and had little to do with any known religious faith or path he had ever encountered. He was nothing but a mere molecule floating in the vastness of the cosmos.

"Do you still wish me to be your Mistress, Steven? Is it still your desire to worship at the altar of flesh and to serve me?"

Steven nodded, his body yearning to cast his gaze upon her one last time before he left for destinations unknown.

"Yes, yes, I would like that, but, where are we? I have no recollection of getting here, wherever here is."

The voice was close by now, its tone alluring and seductive.

"You are where you are supposed to be, Steven, at my side, as per your desire; is this not what you have longed for? Did your path not bring you here of your own free will?"

Steven lowered his head in self-inflicted shame, his failure almost too much to bare and began to weep softly.

"It is the only thing I truly longed for, but despite my best efforts I failed you, Mistress. I failed miserably at the tasks given and as such am not worthy to be allowed by your side. All I ask is for your forgiveness and that you don't think less of me, I couldn't bear the thought of you hating me, it would be worse than death itself."

"Now, now young man, you shouldn't be so harsh on yourself, you didn't fail me at all, in fact, you passed every test with more vigour and strength than any previous slave. You have impressed me and proven your worth."

Steven rubbed his tear stained cheeks and smiled meekly.

"What? but how is that possible?"

A sudden gust of wind alerted him to a presence standing just behind him. He smiled as a waft of beautifully scented perfume caught his nostrils. He felt the sudden exhalation of hot breath against the nape of his neck then words of gratitude whispered softly in his ear.

"It was my intention to send you to the church to see if you could survive when faced with horrific and unearthly odds, for I need only the strong beside me. Of course, you did indeed survive, proving my instincts correct. Your resolve and determination to please me was nothing short of humbling.

"Your second test served two purposes. Firstly, I wanted to make sure your victory wasn't just luck, and secondly, I sent that cowardly traitor Fenston to you as a gift. I wanted you to kill the person who would tear you from my loving embrace, and once again you excelled. I have to say that killing yourself in the process wasn't part of my design, and needn't have happened, but proved your complete loyalty to me none the less."

Steven closed his eyes once again, the blissful tone of her voice freeing him of any lingering doubt or earthly wants.

"What happens now?" he croaked.

"Now? Now we go back, Steven, for I have the power to resurrect those who I deem useful to me, would you like that? To feel the hot sand beneath your feet or the autumnal breeze bite against your exposed cheeks once again? To walk with your head held high whilst those who have shown you nothing but scorn and contempt, grovel on their knees beneath you? I can make you a god amongst men, Steven, all you have to do is say yes, but be warned it comes at a price."

Steven could only nod in compliance.

"Yes, Mistress, more than anything, I long to serve you, but…"

He paused, not wanting to finish the sentence but desperately in need of the answer sought.

"But what, my love? We should have no secrets from each other. Tell me what ails you and I shall cast light and illuminate the way."

He cleared his throat and lowered his gaze.

"But I've never seen you in the flesh, never stood before you, only in my dreams and on the computer screen have you presented yourself to me. I long to touch you is all."

"I understand your frustration, my love, and the path travelled has been a difficult one but now you must rejoice, for the time of our first union is at hand. It is true that you have done all that I have asked, and it is only fair that you are granted a reward for loyal service."

Steven could feel his heart jump, his mind a whirlpool of emotions at the thought of kneeling before her.

"So, by my grace I shall allow you to return, and tomorrow I will grant you a private audience. Together we shall explore the furthest regions of ecstasy and carnal lust. Choose a place and time to meet and I shall be there. You need not contact me for I will know. Now go, for I am bored of this tiresome exchange and have other things to attend to."

Steven felt the presence depart, leaving him alone in the darkness once again. But as he blissfully pondered on the second chance so graciously gifted to him, something caught his attention. He strained his eyesight and could see little speckles of light flashing in the distance, like tiny fireflies busily going about their business on the cusp of human vision. He strained even harder to make out what was happening then realised that the lights were getting closer and increasing in size. Overcome by a sudden rush of fear, Steven flung his arms up to shield his face as the lights began to travel past him, their bodies leaving elongated streaks of vivid colour in their wake, their speed staggering. He began to scream as more lights bombarded him. This time, instead of bypassing, they began to strike him all over his body, their velocity effortlessly carving tunnels through flesh and tissue then exiting from the other side of his torso and his extremities. The wounds allowing puddles of blood to be vented and left to float into the great expanse of nothingness. Steven screwed his eyes tight as the barrage intensified, the damage inflicted causing him to teeter on the edge of losing consciousness. He screamed one last time as the biggest and final light entered his mouth and erupted from the back of his head.

Thirteen

Steven opened his eyes and found himself standing on a desolate and litter swept street. Around him, abandoned cars lay silent, some of which were on fire, sending large plumes of acrid black smoke swirling and twisting into the sky above. He scanned the area and let his weary eyes linger upon the scene of dystopian annihilation surrounding him. Buildings sat silently, decayed and battle damaged. What appeared to be bullet holes peppered the once high-class and expensive façades, their windows smashed, allowing curtains and blinds to swing gently in the breeze. At ground level, shop apertures and entrances lay wide open, the contents of which lay strewn and discarded across the dirty and blood-stained pavements.

As he took a step forward, his shoe gently nudged and dislodged something, the impact of which sent it tumbling along the cracked and worn tarmac with a metallic clatter. He moved towards it, bent over and retrieved the shiny object. He turned his hand over and stretched out his palm to reveal the item. He eyed the empty bullet casing, the metal glinting in the bright sunlight. Steven let out a long steady breath. It was only then he noticed the floor awash with yet more spent .50 calibre casings, the road reduced to nothing more than a sea of blood and brass. He didn't really know anything about guns but had played enough games and seen enough movies to recognise that these were heavy duty rounds, ammunition only used by the military and judging by the amount littering the area, it must have been one hell of a fight.

He suddenly remembered the creatures from the church.

Had they been successful in freeing themselves and escaping their cosmic prison? If so, that would explain the amount of firepower brought to bear, the apparent devastation a testament that the ensuing battle must have been nightmarish. It didn't take a genius to see that the world had indeed changed, but despite Fenston's plan to unleash the ancient ones, and there by, enslaving humanity, Steven felt immensely lucky. Lucky because he alone had been chosen by the Mistress to survive and thrive whilst all others perished or had been transformed into those grotesque creatures. Try as he might he couldn't summon a shred of apathy, after all, it wasn't like he was going to miss anyone or the world as it was. It had never given him anything other than ridicule and heartbreak, and as such, he felt as if he owed it nothing and, in all honesty, would be happy to see it burn to nothing more than ash.

Steven sucked in a laboured breath as it suddenly went dark. He stared at the floor and realised that the sudden drop in light was attributed to a shadow being cast from above. He raised his eyes to witness a colossal creature silently gliding overhead, its dark grey body bulbus and distorted, its size the length of a football field. At its head sat seven monstrous, yet, seemingly alert eyes, each one studiously surveying the ravaged and war-torn streets below. It cast its gaze directly at Steven, its obsidian pupils contracting as if deciding how to proceed, then, as if losing interest in its possible prey, returned its emotionless stare to the direction of travel. As the abomination moved away, Steven noted seven or eight large tentacles swinging gently below its immense body, the ends of which just skimmed the tops of the surrounding buildings as it passed by.

The young survivor held his breath as he realised that he had seen this creature before. His nightmarish visions of a civilisation lying in ruin returning in graphic detail, the all-encompassing feelings of helplessness saturating every fibre of being. But unlike the previous encounter, Steven had since reassessed his motivations and had pushed the boundaries of what he deemed acceptable. In many ways, he had changed for the better, his sense of moral entitlement somewhat warped by his new-found sense of purpose. The purpose of serving his Mistress, leaving all other concerns by the wayside.

Steven remained blissfully stoic as he watched the creature disappear into the distance. Its humungous shape now nothing more than a black smudge on the horizon. He turned to face the setting sun and noted it would soon be dark and thought it prudent to find shelter, especially if Fenston's minions still stalked the streets at night. Of course, there was no way he could go back to his own flat as it would no doubt be lying in ruins, the result of his improvised, yet highly effective detonation. He surveyed the area and grinned when the familiar sight of the five-star hotel he used to pass everyday caught his attention. All twenty-five floors towering into the sky, as if it was a shining beacon, willing him to approach. Perfect he muttered under his breath. Not only would that be a suitable place to rest up and get some sleep, but it could also serve as the most idyllic of locations for his first encounter with his Mistress. Steven gave the area one last scan and started to walk in the direction of the hotel, the distance of a couple of miles a welcome respite from previous events. As he moved forward he couldn't help but whistle a happy tune, for his mood was jubilant and optimistic, his future possibilities limitless.

The two-mile stroll had taken less than an hour and had been relaxingly uneventful, but as he approached the hotel, he noticed something move at the corner of his eye, a fleeting enigma both fast and slimline. He paused and turned, his eyes studying the huge billboard to his left, the large frame and poster happily advertising a new airline service, the smiling hostesses enlarged, and well-manicured face a picture of sophistication and high society. Again, he noticed something move, but this time on the top of the colossal sign. Against the setting sun, he raised his hand and shielded his eyes, and stared at the thing responsible for gaining his attentions. The creature was small, roughly the size of a large dog, but its face was feline in appearance, it's dark grey hairless body thin and skeletal. Steven watched curiously as the monster moved elegantly along the edge of the billboard and crouched down, perched on the edge, its gaze directed at the lone traveller. It hissed vehemently, a row of spines rising from its back and along its previously unseen tail, its eyes a matte black.

Steven stood motionless, his curiosity pinged by such an unusual and vicious looking animal. For some strange reason Steven didn't feel as if he was in danger, he was positive that nothing could stop his destiny and it was as if the Mistress held sway over such horrors and wouldn't let any harm come to her chosen one. The creature hissed again and lifted its rake thin arm. Steven watched as it extended its finger, the wicked looking digit pointing at something on the far side of the road. Steven found himself nodding, as if understanding the gesture, and turned to see what it had alerted him to.

Behind him, and to his right, Steven could see the hotels impressive five-story car park, its design minimalistic, its aesthetic and appearance pleasing, despite its mundane purpose. But it wasn't its everyday features that held Steven's gaze but what adorned its dark stone walls. On every level, and as far as he could see, hung the mutilated cadavers of hundreds of people. Their arms outstretched above them and lashed with barbed wire, all of them attached to rope that had been slung from one end of the floor to the other. Their torsos ripped in two at the waste, their legs and internal organs piled up in huge mounds at ground level and across the well-tended ornamental garden to the front of the structure. Steven stood in awe, the gruesome display a monumental artistic triumph. He took a step forward, intrigued and wanting to inspect further but paused when he remembered his own priorities. He let out a soft sigh, then turned to once again face, whom he presumed, was the architect of the cadaver gallery. He nodded at the stationary creature, its eyes alight with cunning and mischief.

"Are you responsible?" Steven asked softly, unable to hide his approval.

The cat-like thing hissed and squealed then nodded. It began clapping its ravaged hands together and bobbing up and down on the spot, its lower limbs still gripping the thin wooden board. Steven smiled, he too nodded.

"Well, I've got to go now, but keep up the good work."

The monster grinned and let out a high-pitched cackle, then darted along the top of the board, and with amazing agility leapt to an adjoining building. Steven watched its progress until it disappeared into the shadows. He huffed under his breath. What a curious little fellow. He must remember to ask Mistress all about him.

Once the creature was out of his range of vision, he turned and walked towards the plush looking stairwell that led from the guest dropping off point, to the hotel lobby. As he climbed the smooth and elegant steps he once again took in the putrid rotting bodies discarded on the walls, the remains of their tattered clothes flapping gently in the breeze. Oh well, that's what happens when you're not on the winning side. Upon reaching the top, he held on to the handle, and without a second glance, pushed open the heavy gilded and highly ostentatious door.

Mesmerised, Steven gleefully entered the plush looking, and well decorated foyer of the hotel. His eyes immediately drawn to the expensive looking furniture lovingly arranged around the large ornate fountain set in the middle. The steady and tranquil water still bubbling and flowing, its sound adding to the surreal ambience of the abandoned building. He followed the deep and plush carpet to the reception and made his way to the rear of the impressively made wooden counter and eyed the rows of keys hanging on the board. After a few seconds he settled on the luxurious penthouse suite and couldn't help but let out a childlike giggle. The notion of a "nobody" like him having free reign in a five-star hotel somehow amusing, yet socially forbidden. "The rules of the old world no longer hold sway," he found himself stating out loud as he snatched up the key and made his way to the front of the reception area.

Before exploring further, Steven took a few minutes to truly take in his opulent surroundings, after all, it wasn't every day that a mere plebe got to experience such priceless hospitality. He cast his gaze upon expensive looking paintings, no doubt created by some well-known and highly respected artist. The lavish chairs and small reading tables strategically placed around the edges of the impressively sized room. Then finally to the grandiose staircase, its marble steps no doubt intended to entice and impress the wealthy into the luxury so easily afforded and taken for granted. This truly was the most perfect setting for his first encounter, a meeting and joining of two souls destined to be forever entwined.

Steven let out a blissful sigh and heard his stomach unexpectedly give out a low rumble. He rubbed his abdomen and realised he couldn't remember the last time he had actually eaten something, and as such highlighted the fact that his priority should be to head to the kitchen and hopefully rustle up a lavish feast to sooth his rapidly increasing hunger pains.

Steven made his way past the marble staircase and exited the foyer via a staff only door situated to the right, then followed the long low-lit corridor towards, what he believed to be, the kitchen area. He couldn't help but feel smug as he found what he was looking for with relative ease, the anticipation of a hearty meal growing with every step. He stood motionless and looked about the enormously sized industrial room and was secretly impressed by the amount of equipment and utensils lining the white tiled walls, its floor pristine and well maintained.

Steven's stomach let out another mournful groan as the feint waft of previously prepared food teased his nostrils. His gaze fell upon the large heavy metal door of the walk-in fridge at the far end of the room. He noted that this should be his first port of call and moved forward, eager to see what delights lay within. Steven felt the chill wash over him as he tugged the handle and pulled open the door, the sudden blast of cool air somewhat refreshing, soothing his aching muscles. He stepped inside and eyed the rows of fresh food neatly organised on four sets of metal shelving. As he moved further within, he was greeted with the sight of an abundance of delicious looking vegetables, plump fresh fruits and succulent looking slabs of precooked meats, not to mention a host of enticing dairy products. With such a delectable choice, he didn't know where to begin.

Steven slumped back into one of the foyers expensive looking deep filled chairs and stuffed the remnants of his meal into his mouth, wiped his face on his sleeve, and brushed the crumbs from his lap. He smiled at the thought of his actions being frowned upon by those who would normally frequent such an establishment. It had been an hour since first entering the kitchen and had only taken him less than five minutes to decide what his meal of choice should be. He had settled on a few slabs of cold meat, a rather generous helping of pre-cooked pasta mixed with peppers and herbs, topped off with a nice fruit salad. At the time, he had toyed with the idea of having a pudding but was now glad he had opted to go without.

For the second time, Steven looked about him and relaxed into the chair. In his mind's eye he imagined what the hotel would have been like before all this had happened. He envisaged the hustle and bustle of smartly dressed business men and women going about their daily routines, rushing to meetings and making huge decisions regarding vast sums of money; the likes of which normal people would never experience. Then there was the hard working but low paid hotel staff rushing back and forth to satisfy the whims of unappreciative millionaires whilst struggling to feed their own families. Steven grimaced All your money and power didn't save you from what was coming, did it Mr Money maker?

Being a bit of a self-confessed geek, Steven had often tried to imagine what the end of the world would look like and how it would happen. In fact, he had spent more than many an hour trying to figure out the answer. Would it be the result of thermal nuclear war or some airborne military grade pathogen, accidently released by some top-secret government facility? Being an avid gamer, he had always taken part in discussions on gamer forums regarding the likelihood of a Zombie apocalypse, but in his opinion, that had been highly unlikely and nothing more than a Hollywood fairy-tale. However, not once did he contemplate that the end would come via some chaotic unseen void, full of hungry and horrific monsters that enjoyed nothing more than ripping flesh from bone. Nope, certainly didn't see that one coming!

Over the past few days Steven had seen things he never thought possible. At first, and with good reason, he had been terrified, but now felt liberated by the whole experience. In a world full of millions of people, he alone had been chosen by some otherworldly deity. To sit at her side and rebuild what had been lost, to raise a new dawn of humanity from the ruins of the fallen civilisation. Yes indeed, to say he was proud was an understatement and he couldn't wait to get started.

Steven turned and faced the main entrance of the lobby and noted it was now dark, which was strange as he hadn't noticed the receding light. He shrugged and made his way to the doorway and began to drag a large three-seater sofa across the threshold, a makeshift barrier should anything with nefarious intent venture too close. Satisfied, he made his way across the reception room, up the marble stairs and headed towards the lift. He pressed the button and was greeted by a soft pinging sound followed by the swish as the double doors opened, allowing him to enter the small but posh looking facility. He jabbed his finger at the penthouse button and could feel the excitement building as the doors closed, a soothing voice announcing his destination through the lift's intercom. With a soft judder the lift began its ascent, the split-second feeling of weightlessness giving him a feeling of nervousness, the remnants of a childhood trauma. He shook his head, not wanting to recall such pointless and unwanted memories.

As soon as the doors opened, Steven moved quickly into the brightly lit hallway, his desire to see his new lodgings filling him with giddy jubilation. He looked both left and right and noted that there seemed to be only four rooms on the entire floor, three of which, he assumed, to be second only to the penthouse suit in opulence. Steven glanced at the sign on the wall opposite, the gold coloured and elegant bold font proudly stating that the room he required was to his right and was situated at the far end of the hall. The weary young man looked to his feet and was surprised to see that, instead of the usual, and expected thick carpet, the floor was lined with beautiful marble slabs, the craftsmanship of which was simply stunning. Steven gave a chuckle as he made his way towards his suite, a slight spring in his step adding to the growing excitement.

As he reached his door, he retrieved the key from his pocket and with a trembling hand, slipped it into the lock. With a pronounced click the security measure disengaged allowing its guest to enter. Steven paused, pushed open the door, and took a step over the threshold.

Fourteen

Steven stood silently and with unreserved reverence, his body shaking slightly, his eyes fixated on the scene from his suite window. He couldn't find the words to describe what his panoramic view afforded him. He felt somewhat blessed, for from his vantage point he could see the city below him in all its glory. In another time, the obscenely wealthy would have paid thousands for the slightest of glimpses of the sights granted him, but now Steven alone had the honour of witnessing the savage and painful birth of a new age taking place as he watched from his lofty position.

Stretching into the distance, and in all directions, Steven could see billowing smoke and torturous flames rising from a thousand fires, each raging and consuming everything around them, their insatiable hunger releasing great plumes of ash and smoke into the blackened sky. In amongst the putrid and choking fumes, Steven could see faint movement, what he believed to be a large flock of birds; their movements agile and elegant. But as the darkened gathering got closer, Steven realised that they were not birds at all, but rather, thousands of vulture sized creatures twisting and turning, their bodies wormlike and what looked like four spindly and jagged legs, reaching out from behind a circular shaped mouth. He stared in wonderment as the wingless creatures still found the powers of flight and began attacking each other, their vicious looking teeth snapping and biting.

Steven watched them for over ten minutes, their aerial display hypnotic, their formations mesmerizing. Then, without warning, they began swooping towards the ground, their acceleration dizzying, before disappearing, their earthly-bound actions hidden by manmade buildings and concrete creations. Steven had witnessed horrors, but these were unlike any he had seen before. These somehow seemed to be of a more unspeakable and hideous nature, their squirming bodies a mass of teeth, scrawny legs and what appeared to be random human limbs jutting out from their main bodies, serving no real purpose but to intimidate those still living. Gory trophies of mankind's decent into chaos. In the gloomy streets below, Steven could see yet more abominations, some crawling on all fours, others on two feet, all of which snarled and snapped as they scavenged and sought out fresh prey amongst the ruins.

A sudden scream caught Steven by surprise. He tore his attention away from the flying plights and rested his eyes on a small van parked just on the very edges of his scope of vision. He strained in the gloom to see what was happening, then held his breath in anticipation. He saw four spider-like creatures drag a scared young woman, no older than twenty and dressed in filthy rags, from her hiding place beneath the vehicle and toss her mercilessly into the road. The tormented woman screamed and pleaded for her life but was silenced as the four monsters were joined, out of the shadows, by another three, all of which lunged forward and began to devour her. Her screams lasted mere seconds as the beasts made easy work of her flesh and bones, the remnants of their efforts staining the road around them with a torrent of blood and human remains. As quickly as it had started, the creatures finished their meal and slowly skulked away, continuing with their search for yet more meat to consume.

Steven stepped back from the window. He felt sick, not sick with disgust but sick with excitement. The scenes playing out had little effect other than turning him on both sexually and psychologically. They say change is painful, so who was he to argue with such astute logic. Steven gathered his thoughts and gently closed the curtains, ignoring the fresh wave of screams echoing from the streets below. He smiled and headed for the bathroom, slipping off his jumper and t-shirt as he manoeuvred himself around the expensive furniture that dotted the luxury abode.

After finishing his shower and using the fresh razor and foam he found in the bathroom, Steven wrapped himself in a towel and padded back into the main living area. He stared at his tattered and bloodstained clothing lying discarded on the floor. He chuckled at the sight of his soiled clothing. No way he could meet his Mistress dressed in those he muttered. He briskly did an about turn then casually ambled to the wardrobe. To his surprise, he found three sets of freshly cleaned and diligently pressed clothing lovingly hung up. Steven couldn't help but think that this was just another sign that he was indeed travelling the road of pure destiny. He pulled out a dark blue cotton shirt and held it to his body and smiled when the size seemed to be correct, the fabric feeling soft and expensive in his hands.

He then proceeded to select a suitable pair of dark grey trousers, which were a size too big, but he reckoned that with the belt supplied they would suffice and be more than adequate for the purpose intended. As his eyes fell to the floor, he was greeted by two pairs of highly polished black shoes. He slipped a pair on and almost laughed out loud. What were the chances of them being his size, yet to his personal amusement and relief, they were?

The young office worker dried himself, dressed and stood before the full-length mirror inspecting his new self. He nodded his approval, his dapper new look making him feel every part the God he now knew himself to be. The shadow of the old Steven nothing but a distant and insignificant memory lost to the annals of time and space.

Steven was tempted to once again look out of the window but was suddenly hit by a wave of exhaustion, and to be honest it didn't come as a surprise, after all, he had died and been reborn. Obviously, he would need to catch up on some well-deserved sleep. He took off his clothes and set them down neatly on the small two-seater couch then made his way to the king-size bed.

Regardless of his previous routines, he was not inclined to inspect the small clock situated on the sideboard. Time held no meaning in this new world, it was nothing but a man-made construction, to which, all had no choice but to be enslaved. He joyfully climbed into his bed and pulled the soft, fresh duvet over his body, the material giving him a sense of refined comfort and security. As his head lay on the pillow, his mind wandered to his imminent meeting. He closed his eyes, the thought of his Mistress soothing his clawing fragility. No sooner had he done so, he immediately felt himself descending into a dreamless sleep, the haunting ambience of the nothingness simply divine.

Outside his window the silence was once again shattered by the distant screams of people falling prey to the creatures that hid in the shadows. Despite the chorus of misery and suffering, Steven did not stir, in fact, it was probably the best sleep he had ever had.

Steven gradually opened his eyes and stretched his arms, his body trying to adjust itself back to the waking hours and dislodge the welcoming embrace of sleep. He yawned, threw the duvet back and swung his legs out of bed. He felt fantastic. He couldn't believe, not just the amount, but the quality of sleep he had been gifted. Not only his body, but his mind felt refreshed and ready for whatever lay ahead. As he sat on the edge of the bed he couldn't help but look, this time he took the opportunity to inspect the clock, not because it held any real sway, but because he wanted to know how long he had to wait for his Mistress to arrive. The bright fluorescent digits read 11:12. Steven couldn't believe that it was so late in the day. In times gone by, he would be lucky if he slept in past seven thirty.

He scratched his head and got to his feet, his toes happily exploring the deep pile carpet. He had decided to set the meeting for 2 pm. That way he would have enough time to prepare himself and make the room look nice. Not that he thought the state of the room would have any bearing on his future regarding the joining of two souls, but because he reckoned, he should at least try and make an effort. After all, he now had an image to maintain and everybody knows the ladies like a well-presented man. He was still unsure how the Mistress would know the allotted time, but quickly dismissed the thought for fear of her taking offence. All he could do was to trust in her powers, after all, she had brought him back from the dead.

Steven spent the next two hours exploring the other rooms of the hotel. In one he found a nice bouquet of beautifully scented flowers, in another, a box of expensive Belgian chocolates. He transported it all to his suite, and strategically placed them to make her feel comfortable and to bid her welcome. He then ventured back to the kitchen and decided to gather a selection of nibbles should she have an appetite. A buffet of off-cut meats and savoury bites should suffice. He even managed to find some individually wrapped mini cheesecakes to act as desert.

Whilst investigating the deepest depths of the hotel Steven stumbled upon, then decided to use, a hostess trolley to ferry his romantic horde back to the top floor. To his delight, managed to fit it all in his mini fridge. He had even managed to secure a three-thousand-pound bottle of Champagne from the hotel bar to mark the occasion. After adding the finishing touches to the room and ironing his clothes for the second time, Steven had another shower and got dressed, then sat on his bed, eagerly awaiting her arrival.

As he quickly glanced at the digital clock, he began to feel the soothing sensation of inevitability, for as the clock changed to 2 pm he heard the distinctive ping of the lift's arrival, then the echo of high heels traversing the marble flooring. He jumped to his feet, ran his hand through his shaggy mop of hair and made his way to his hotel room door.

Stuart R Brogan

Fifteen

Present Day:

Steven lowered his head yet again and hesitated. His bravado all but gone, lost to a chasm of wanton servitude. The Mistress eyed him with vehemence, her posture relaxed yet threatening.

"I said, come to me," she repeated sternly.

Steven gingerly moved towards her, his ego not wanting to upset or cause offence, the fear of acting inappropriately causing him to fumble his words and actions. The Mistress remained motionless, the shine of her latex dress glinting in the sunlight streaming through the large window behind her. Steven managed to look up and once again could feel the swell of excitement surging through his body, her sublime beauty radiating and filling the room.

"Well? You have longed for this moment for so long, now when it finally arrives you act like some love-sick child, yearning for acceptance and adulation? If this is not your desire, and you are not prepared to play by the rules, I shall gather my things and leave. I have no time to play such petty games with weak-minded fools. If you are to worship me then you must give yourself unto me in the entirety. Accept my will as the only thing that truly matters. To have you come this far, then fall by the wayside would be a waste of time for both you, and I."

Upon hearing her threat to leave, Steven quickened his pace, he stopped two feet in front of her, his body trembling. She smirked and eyed him with delectable scorn.

"Good boy, slave, you are beginning to know your place. Now get down and kneel before me, give all that you possess and offer unwavering worship at the altar of flesh."

The young man bent down and knelt before his Mistress, the smell of her perfume beginning to reach his nostrils. He moved his eyes without moving his head and could see the highly polished patent black heels just in front of his face, her feet encased in black stockings. He sucked in a ravaged breath as he awaited his next command but suddenly heard unexpected movement emanating from behind his Mistress. He quickly glanced up, his momentary curiosity over riding the need to remain subservient, just in time to see the feline like creature from the carpark slowly emerge from behind the couch. Its pincer like claws pulling itself up the plush material until it reached the top. It turned and relaxed back on its haunches, its orblike eyes watching his every move. As Steven lowered his gaze it let out a raspy cackle, as if approving of his decision to look away.

"Oh, don't worry about him, if anything, it's me you should be concerned with. He is nothing but a pet, a loyal one, but a pet none the less."

Steven felt the tip of her shoe against his chin, then a slight pressure as she used her foot to force his head upwards.

"I expect my slaves to be strong when I wish it, to bend to my will when I demand it, and in return for such loyalty I shall impart great rewards. Do you understand and accept, Steven? Or do you wish to return to the doldrum that was your pointless existence before I so graciously took you under my wing? Or better yet, would you like to be my pet's new art project?" The creature let out another hiss, followed by a sinister laugh as if willing Steven to surrender his body freely to its artistry of woe.

Steven nodded, and croaked his reply.

"I understand and accept, Mistress. I am yours to do with as you please."

The Mistress began to laugh, something in her tone seemed wicked and malicious.

"Then stand and remove your clothes, for I intend to inspect what my divine mercy has purchased, and all being well I shall school you in the pleasures of the flesh."

Steven rose to his feet and began to unbutton his shirt. The Mistress smiled as the garment fell to the floor, then chuckled softly as Steven removed his trousers and pants, leaving him standing naked in front of her. She looked him up and down with appraising eyes, then with a sudden movement reached out and took his growing erection in her hand. Steven tensed as he felt her finger nails rip into his shaft, blood began to gently flow from the wounds. He closed his eyes, willing her to increase her movements and anticipating the relief when he ejaculated. Instead, he was shocked when he felt her let go, leaving him shaking with expectation.

"I don't think so, not yet," she chuckled.

Confused and naked, the vulnerable man suddenly felt a massive blow to the back of his head, the impact causing him to fall forward and land on the floor with a heavy thump. Through blurred and swimming vision, he could see two figures gather around him, their features distorted and unrecognisable, then muffled voices followed by discordant laughter as he slowly slipped into unconsciousness.

Sixteen

The sudden and forceful punch to his face, snapped Steven clear of his unexpected and pain induced slumber. He tried to move but found his head lolling uselessly back and forth, his eye balls threatening to roll back into their sockets and disappear completely due to the residual pressure. He began to cough, the sudden and abrasive movement causing a bloodied mix of saliva and phlegm to fall from his mouth and land on his chest, the after effects of such a brutal assault resonating in his skull. Around him, the sensation of overwhelming and oppressive heat clawed relentlessly at his battered body, leaving his skin clammy and wet. He tried to ignore the discomfort and sucked in a lungful of air as to kick start his recovery, but instead, felt a sudden surge of pain as if his organs were drenched in liquid fire.

In his state of sudden panic, Steven attempted to get to his feet, but quickly gave up when he realised his ankles were securely lashed to the legs of a chair. He went to move his arms, but again found them tightly bound and unmovable. Slowly, his eyesight returned. Hazy at first then clearer. He looked about him to try to ascertain his location but could see nothing that would indicate this, nor give him answers. The room itself cloaked in almost impenetrable darkness. Upon his body, and around the room, he could feel, and hear, the continuous drips of moisture falling from the ceiling. Its hypnotic and rhythmic sound adding to the oppressive subterranean atmosphere.

Steven lowered his head, and through the gloom could just make out his bruised and naked body, the skin itself covered in filth, scatterings of dried blood, and a shimmering layer of sweat.

"What the fuck is happening!" he screamed, struggling against his restraints, the size of the room echoing his baritone, yet understandably nervous voice.

The chair bound captive waited for the resonation to subside and strained to hear any movement. He was greeted by only silence. He screamed for a second time, and yet again no answer came forth from the darkness.

"What the fuck do you want from me? Who are you?" he bellowed.

There was a soft chuckle from behind followed by a female voice mimicking his question in a childlike tone. Steven tried to turn and face his tormentor, his bondage preventing all but the slightest movement. The young man took in another laboured breath, the heat seemingly growing in intensity and beginning to make him feel unresponsive and groggy. Steven was suddenly aware of a figure moving slowly to his left and could just make out a human silhouette passing through the room's grim interior. He squinted to get a better look but couldn't make out any features. The figure stopped in front of him approximately seven feet away, its breathing audible yet its identity still hidden from view. The bound young man let his chin fall to his chest and began to sob quietly, his tears causing clean strips to appear on his dirt encrusted body.

"Please, please, just tell me what you want. Who are you? What have I done to deserve this? Where is my Mistress?"

Once again there was another subdued cackle, wheezy and hoarse.

"What does it matter? The world around us has gone to shit, nothing is like it was and never will be again. Your so-called Mistress obviously doesn't give a fuck about you, so why shouldn't I be allowed to have a little fun before those creatures get to me and rip me to shreds like countless others?"

"I, I, don't know what to say. I'm just a nobody, a normal man, what could I have possibly done to warrant this treatment? What have I done to you? If you're going to kill me then just get on with it, stop with the fucking mind games and finish me off." He paused and raised his head in an attempt to make eye contact with his captor, his hopes of facilitating escape diminishing with each passing second.

"I have nothing to live for now anyway. She has left me. I am no longer worthy of her affections. I deserve to be abandoned, cast out like the pathetic failure I am."

There was a brief pause. Steven could hear his captor's shallow breathing, it too, obviously affected by the humidity in the room.

"Aaaahhhh, how sad and yet so very noble of you, but maybe I don't want to finish you off so quickly. Perhaps I want to take my time and enjoy every moment, maybe that's the only pleasure left open to me in this world lying in ruins and flames. Why should I deny myself a little fun before I too join the millions that have already perished thanks to your selfish and inhumane actions? Why should I grant an animal such as you any degree of mercy when the blame rests solely on your shoulders for what has happened to humanity?"

Steven couldn't answer or think of a single reason why his captor shouldn't carry out her threats. It was true, it was all his fault. It was him who had angered the ancient ones and let them escape. It was him who had unleashed Fenston and his creations upon the world. The end of days lay squarely at his feet, and for that, he needed to be punished, to pay for his egotistical transgressions.

"Just, just, do it. I don't care anymore, finish it and send me straight to hell if that's what will make you feel better, to feel as if justice has been served, to be able to sleep at night with a clear conscience."

"Sleep? Sleep? How the fuck can anyone sleep when all around us those creatures are hunting, never resting, always searching for their next meal!" The voice was increasing in volume, threatening to become a torrent of rage. Once again, the room fell silent, the only sounds were of the two occupants breathing, both shallow and withdrawn.

"Why did you do it, Steven? Why did you release them from their prison? What makes a small time nobody like you want to see the world fall? I can only surmise that life has treated you unfairly. Hell, it might even have fucked you in ways I couldn't possibly imagine nor understand, but so many innocent lives have been taken, Steven. The very future of our species erased from history, and for what? Maybe you are bereft of any form of conscience, thereby not much caring for the fate of others."

The young man began to chuckle, his mind beginning to show signs of breaking in to a million pieces under the continuous psychological torture.

"If you want the truth, and because your gonna kill me anyway, it wasn't me who released them, it was Fenston. He's the one you need to be having this conversation with, not me. Sure, I went to the church with the whole-hearted intention of killing some so-called innocent people, just because my Mistress commanded it, but when I got there, the plan went to shit, and they fucking turned on me, they changed into those nightmares," he began to sob again. "I barely made it out of there alive," he added sombrely.

The rooms silence was suddenly broken by an almighty cheer, the four walls resonating with the sound of mellifluous laughter and lively joviality. Steven looked about him but still couldn't make out those responsible, his senses overwhelmed by the intense explosion of emotions and the unexpected revelries. He squinted and turned his head, clenching his eyes tight as the room was abruptly flooded with blinding white light. He kept them shut and counted down from ten, convinced that he was about to die. When he reached zero, and found himself still alive, he let out a cautious and steady breath, his relief audible. Fearing an imminent attack, he gently opened them, his body primed to take any number of vicious blows from his unknown assailants.

Steven looked on in disbelief as he let every detail of his location sink in. He blinked myopically as he slowly scanned the interior of The Horny Toad. Its walls were decaying and paintwork peeling, its wooden bar ravaged and scarred by what looked like deep claw marks, its bare floorboards scattered with spent bullet casings cast amongst pools of stagnant blood. He turned his gaze to the ceiling and gagged at the sight above him. The roof itself was covered in a plethora of human body parts, each rotten piece secured to the structure of the building by large rusting masonry nails. He quickly turned away, not wishing to acknowledge what he had seen and began to scan the rest of the room. To his left he could see the pictures he had so lovingly stared at and admired when he first visited hanging lop sided, their frames smashed, the glass shattered into tiny pieces. It was then he noticed the lone female figure standing motionless before him.

Steven sucked in a deep breath as the overweight figure of Chloe Hargreaves ambled towards him, her face a picture of sadistic amusement, her eyes alive with delight.

"How? What the..." Steven muttered as his former boss bent forward and with one hand grabbed his cheek and began to wiggle it, as if playing with a child.

"Surprise!" she sniggered, enjoying watching the look of confusion on her plaything's face.

Steven began to shake his head in denial, desperately willing her to be a figment of his rapidly fragmented imagination.

"Bet ya didn't see that one coming, did ya, loser?" she added as she straightened up.

Steven began to whimper, the realisation that he had been played crushing his ego and shattering what little of his masculinity remained. He glared at the fat woman.

"What the hell are you?"

Chloe smiled and shrugged.

"Does it really matter? Don't you find labels so restrictive? Why does everything need to be pigeon holed, to have a name thrust upon it so others may identify it and convince others of its validity. Why can't we just be, to just exist, and be able to go about our daily business without the confines of labels?"

"No more games, what are you?" he rasped.

"Um, well Steven, that's a bit of a loaded question." She glanced over his shoulder and directed her question to the stranger entering Steven's field of vision.

"Well? What am I?"

Steven turned to his right just as Fenston came into view. He was dressed in his normal dapper attire, his hair and beard neatly trimmed and manicured just as Steven remembered it. He nodded a greeting at the younger man and smiled.

"Why good evening, Sir. I trust you are keeping well and that you are in good spirits? I would offer you a drink but I'm afraid all this end of the world stuff has played havoc with our deliveries." Both he and Chloe began to laugh. Steven looked on, unable to respond.

Fenston stopped laughing and stared at his captive, his demeaner changing, an air of menace began to permeate the very air within the bar.

"Now Steven, it's time to get serious I'm afraid. I have to say that stabbing me with a broken dinner plate and blowing me up in a gas explosion was no way to treat a trusted and loyal friend. As such, I believe you owe me an apology, not to mention a new suit." He turned to face Chloe and shrugged his shoulders. "And let's not forget the five pounds for your first pint and a tenner for the taxi fare."

It was Steven's turn to laugh. His head rolled forward as tears began to stream from his eyes, his airways struggling and threatening to hyperventilate. He kept going, the insanity of the situation causing him to convulse and shake. Chloe took a step forward and cocked her head, bemused by the bound man's reaction.

"What's so funny, Steven? Why don't you let us in on the joke?"

Steven glared at his captors.

Goddess

"Now I get it, do you think I'm stupid? well I can see right through you, don't you see, this is all an elaborate charade, a test from my Mistress, this is part of her plan to test my loyalty. Well, the joke's on you. For a second, I admit, you had me going, and yes, I was scared. But any minute now she will walk through that door and release me, at which time we shall be together at last. I know she sent you, you've had your fun, now you can let me go. We are all on the same team."

Steven felt an icy breeze touch his skin, the sudden drop in temperature causing his arm hair to rise. He let out a deep sigh, his breath visible around him and remained stoic as Chloe edged forward, and as she did so started to transform. Steven sat speechless as her hair began to grow longer before his very eyes, the colour changing from light blonde to jet black in a matter of seconds. Her body began to twitch, her limbs stretching to such a degree that the room echoed with the sound of breaking bones. He kept watching as her skin rippled then began to rip causing the torso to somehow dislodge large deposits of fat, dumping it uselessly on the dirty flooring about them. The effect of this gave her an hour glass figure. As she got closer he could see her facial features transmogrify until she was completely different from the Chloe he knew and despised. His captor came to a halt just a few feet in front of him, and through incredulous eyes he looked upon the seductive and familiar image of his Mistress. He held his breath, and in that instant, his world came crashing down around him. She smiled warmly and began to address him but despite her appearance, when she spoke, it was the voice of Chloe that Steven heard.

"I am your Mistress, Steven. I always have been. I've been watching you since the day you were born. Every calamity and failure in your life has been down to me. Every heartbreak you've suffered, every misfortune endured, every stroke of bad luck that has happened to you was because I commanded it. I hate to be the bearer of ill tidings, but you are not the chosen one Steven. You never have been and never will be. You are nothing but a simple roll of the dice, a momentary distraction from the drudgery of immortality, it could have just as easily been someone else. These last few days have been nothing but a temporary amusement for me. Like a child using a magnifying glass to torture ants for no other reason but for pleasure. Your existence is an annoyance to me. In fact, your entire world is like an itch that must be scratched. I was born at a time when the void consumed all, and where there is nothing, we are forced to find our own source of amusement and entertainment. Your life is but a passing nanosecond compared to mine and I must say I've enjoyed it immensely." She paused and smiled a wicked smile. "Rest assured that it's not just the world that hates you, Steven."

She winked and blew him a kiss

"It's the whole fucking universe!"

Again, both Chloe and Fenston began to laugh hysterically. Their bodies writhing and jiggling with hilarity. Steven sighed, his mind resided to his impending death.

"So, what are you then? Some sort of alien being or a power-hungry deity?"

Chloe turned to face him.

"Well, aren't we the inquisitive little lab rat. Since you asked so politely, I shall impart some wisdom. I am older than both, yet neither. I am one of seven that traverse, not only space, but time and reality. Despite what your kind believe, there are too many realities to count. Some beautiful, where dreams come true and all beings are equal and living in harmony. Then there are those that are full of horrors, horrors that would send a man insane with the briefest of looks. Some might say that they would make what's been unleashed here on your world look positively cute and cuddly."

Steven remained silent, his gaze never leaving the woman before him.

"It's funny that you should mention deities, for all that I have ever met, fear us, and with good reason. As for the thousands of races in the universe, they silently pray we don't visit them and tend to give us a wide berth. But it's not all doom and gloom, for I go where I please and do whatever takes my fancy at any given time."

She opened her arms and gestured at the expanse of the room.

"Believe it or not, I have lived in this world for a thousand years, but I have to tell you, I am now, so very bored and wish to move on to some other place. But as a parting gift I have let some of my pets have free reign. In fact, I dare say that ninety percent of the world's population have now been either, converted or, more than likely, have met with a very repugnant and grisly demise, either way, and in complete honesty, I don't much care."

Steven nodded towards Fenston who was stood quietly at the bar, his hand somehow nursing a freshly pulled pint. Fenston noticed Steven's attentive stare and in response raised his glass, tipped his head and smiled broadly. Steven scowled and returned his attention to the Mistress.

"What's his story? Is he one of your pets?"

Chloe glanced at the barman and nodded.

"Why of course, and what a good little boy he is, too, but he is not the only one who longs to serve me, in fact, would you like to meet some of my other pets, Steven? I just know they are dying to meet you."

The room around him was suddenly filled with ecstatic commotion, eager voices chattering and engaging in playful banter. To his rear, Steven began to hear dozens of footsteps scuffing at the debris littered floor as people entered from the street above. He watched stoically as the decimated bar began to fill with a steady throng, some of whom he recognised, others nothing more than strangers. He looked around as the ever-growing crowd nudged and jostled their way into a semi-circle before him, each eager for the bound man to see them in all their glory.

Steven scanned the faces. To his left was the grime encrusted and dishevelled homeless man he had met when he first entered the bar. Next to him stood all his co-workers, each dressed smartly and grinning. One even took the opportunity to give a little wave, their excitement evident. To his right stood his own mother and father, their arms entwined yet not paying Steven any heed, instead, gazing lovingly at Chloe. In the centre, just behind the cause of his ruination stood the Vicar from the church, his robes spotlessly clean. Flanking him, his attentive congregation. His heart sank as he heard yet more footsteps, a deluge of others joining the parade. And so, it went on; school friends; casual acquaintances; his childhood doctor; his first girlfriend, the list was never ending. Everybody he had ever known now stood before him, the bar crowded with smiling and excited faces. Chloe moved towards him, gently rested her hand on his shoulder and whispered soothingly in his ear, her voice delectable.

"I know, I know. It's all rather depressing to find out that your whole life was nothing more than a momentary source of amusement, a passing whim for an otherwise uninterested party." She turned to the crowd who were waiting patiently for their Mistress to address them, their eyes glinting with expectation. Chloe cleared her throat and clasped her hands together.

"Firstly, I would like to thank you all for your hard work and participation, and for making this a truly fun filled last few days. It really does mean a lot to me. You have all conducted yourself with utmost professionalism and with boundless enthusiasm, and as a reward, I hereby decree that all you guys can go forth and kill as many of his kind as you see fit."

There was a muffled chorus of thanks and appreciation, then a hushed silence fell upon the bar once again.

"Just remember that we are only here for a few more days before most of us must leave, but rest assured, I intend that some of you shall be left behind to make sure these humans don't repopulate."

The Mistress returned her attention to the naked and sobbing figure sitting quietly in the chair and smiled warmly.

"Come now everyone, I think Steven deserves a round of applause for being a bloody good sport."

The room erupted with applause, strangers and friends alike began to high five each other, others giving slaps of congratulations on their neighbour's backs. As the revelry ensued, the mistress crouched so she was level with Steven. She eyed him coldly as he raised his head to meet her gaze.

"Thank you, Steven. I truly mean it. Thank you for putting a momentary smile on my face, for giving me a spark of joy amongst the bleakness of the nothingness. It's been a blast."

Before he could think of some heroic retort, the minions crowding the room suddenly began to shudder, their faces and bodies showing symptoms of abhorrent transformation. Their clothes violently ripped from their bodies as moist and discoloured flesh was cleaved open by a thousand-barbed retractile erupting from within. Their sleek frames slithering and entwining with each other.

Steven watched as fountains of blood and putrid internal organs showered the ceiling, some of which fell as a crimson mist upon the scene of horror, adding to the increasingly frenzied bloodlust. He held his breath as the stench of rotten meat and exposed cadavers enveloped his senses, causing his stomach to wretch violently. Each creature began letting out desperate moans as they continued to morph, their remaining human limbs splitting and snapping, the last remnants of humanity lost to a maelstrom of carnage and butchery. Steven gently closed his eyes and silently said a prayer as he saw the wall of hellish detestation close in around him, their growls guttural and savage, their teeth and tendrils dripping with saliva and gore.

Amongst the carnage, the Mistress gave one last smile as her horde fell upon her stricken and defenceless plaything, and even though he meant nothing to her, she was impressed he didn't scream.

Author Bio

Former nightclub Bouncer and unwaveringly proud Heathen who loves nothing more than expanding people's minds with Pagan related Non-Fiction or blowing people's brains out with fast paced, gut wrenching Horror / Thrillers.

Harley lover, extreme metal drummer and avid movie nerd, Stuart has never followed the crowd but instead carved his own path and danced to his own tune. Since his early years Stuart found escapism in both the written word and the silver screen. A huge fan of 80's Action / Horror movies such as The Thing, Aliens, Predator & Die Hard and literary heroes such as Shaun Hutson, Clive Barker. Richard Layman and Brian Lumley, Stuart endeavors to bring an unapologetic cinematic eye to his fiction in the hopes of rekindling his childhood sense of wonder, all whilst blowing through vast amounts of ammunition down his local shooting range.

Stuart currently resides in Glastonbury, UK with his long-suffering Wife and man-eating Shih-Poo dog "Poppy" where he co-owns a kick ass Viking / Asatru shop, fiercely named "Shield Maiden"

J Ellington Ashton Press
presents:
WET WORKS
CONCEPT BY
JIM GOFORTH
TRIGGERED
DUAL DEPRAVITY
VOLUME TWO
DANI BROWN &
DAVID OWAIN HUGHES
CIRCLE JERK
CATT DAHMAN
KETAMINE PANDAS
WARNING
THE QUEEN OF FILTH
DANI BROWN
FESTIVAL OF THE FLESH
JIM GOFORTH
www.jellingtonashton.com
All titles available through Amazon

Made in the
USA
Lexington, KY